LOVE IS WHERE YOU FIND IT

ANGELO THOMAS CRAPANZANO

Copyright © 2017 by Angelo Thomas Crapanzano.

All rights reserved. No part of this publication may be reproduced, distributed, or transmitted in any form or by any means, including photocopying, recording, or other electronic or mechanical methods, without the prior written permission of the publisher, except in the case of brief quotations embodied in critical reviews and certain other noncommercial uses permitted by copyright law. For permission requests, write to the publisher, addressed "Attention: Permissions Coordinator," at the address below.

BookVenture Publishing LLC
1000 Country Lane Ste 300
Ishpeming MI 49849
www.bookventure.com
Hotline: 1(877) 276-9751
Fax: 1(877) 864-1686

Ordering Information:
Quantity sales. Special discounts are available on quantity purchases by corporations, associations, and others. For details, contact the publisher at the address above.

Printed in the United States of America.

Library of Congress Control Number		2017941454
ISBN-13:	Softcover	978-1-64069-054-7
	Pdf	978-1-64069-059-2
	ePub	978-1-64069-060-8
	Kindle	978-1-64069-061-5

Rev. date: 05/02/2017

CONTENTS

DEDICATION

I am dedicating this book in the memory of Lorna Phares, a sweet, gentle and loving lady. Though God has taken her from us she will never be forgotten. May God's loving arms embrace her for eternity.

CHAPTER ONE

A Time for Charity

The typical odor filled the hallways and filtered into all the rooms. John hated it as it reminded him of the time he spent there with his mother. Her heart was worn out and she was too old for a transplant. Now he had to experience a serious problem with his wife. He sat in the waiting room wondering what the doctors would tell him. However, he was sure of the outcome. They had asked him to leave her room while they examined her. The doctors had been called because her blood pressure had dropped to a dangerous level. She had a bad liver. She had contacted hepatitis C and they didn't know about it until it was too late. She needed a liver transplant. However, he was told that she needed a very rare type and it was almost impossible to find. He sat trying to keep his mind off the almost certain results. His mind wondered back to the odor that permeated the hallways of the hospital. He wondered what the odor was. Did it come from standard hospital disinfection alcohol? Was it cleaning fluid used to clean the rooms and floors? A voice suddenly snapped him from his thoughts.

"Hi Dad, how are you holding up?"

"Sarah, honey, what are you doing here?"

"I thought you would need someone to be with you."

"How did you find out about this? I have been trying to keep this from you until I knew for sure what would happen. I just found out today that they would not be able to get a liver for her."

"Daddy, did you forget that I am a doctor? I have ways of finding out these things. Dad, I've been on top of this from the beginning when you first brought her in for tests."

I should have known. Honey, I'm so glad that you're here. I don't think I can handle this by myself."

"How long have you been out here?" asked Sarah.

"I've been out here for about an hour."

"That's too long. Let me go see what is going on." She was about to leave the room when the nurse walked in.

"What is going on with Mrs. Cane?" Sarah asked the nurse.

"The doctor took her down stairs for some tests," she answered. "They should be up soon." No sooner had she finished talking that the doctor walked in. A cold chill ran through John's spine as the doctor walked towards them. What frightened John the most was the sad look on the doctor's face.

"Hi, you must be Doctor Cane" he said to Sarah. "I'm Doctor Brant."

"Hi Doctor Brant," responded Sarah. "This is my father."

"How are you Mr. Cane?" he said shaking his hand. "I'm afraid I have bad news for you. We ran all the tests and found that her liver has ceased to function. That has caused all her organs to start shutting down. We tried all the procedures and drugs we knew and couldn't even slow down the process. I'm so sorry that I couldn't help her." After the first shock wore off Sarah responded.

"How much time does she have?"

"Well I think she will hang on for about two or three days, however the problem is that she may only be conscious for a few hours. So go to her now if you want to talk with her. She is in her room." John and Sarah held back their emotions until the doctor left the room. Then they both hugged and began crying. After a few minutes Sarah pulled away.

"Dad we had better go to her. We want to spend as much time as we can while she is awake. She is probably wondering what happened to her family." Without a word John got up and followed her.

"Let's muster up all the energy and control we can and not let her see our pain. We want her last days to be as pleasant as we can make them."

"OK," said John, "I'll try my best." As they entered the room Annie noticed them and spoke out with a weak voice that was barely audible.

"There you are John, I thought you got lost." Then seeing Sarah, she continued, "Sarah sweetheart. It's so good to see you." Sarah bent down and kissed her mother.

"I'm glad to be here," responded Sarah tears showing in her eyes.

"Now you guys listen to me," said Annie. "I've had a very beautiful life. God has been so good to me. He has given me you two and all the love a woman can hope for."

"Don't talk like that," said Sarah. "We want you to fight to get well, do you hear?"

"Honey I know as well as you, that I only have a little while. I'm looking forward to being with the Lord. The only regret I have is that I don't like leaving your father alone. Let's not waste the time I have in wishful thinking. Let's talk about the good times we had. John, do you remember the time we spent in Florida?" John couldn't control his feelings any longer. He bent over and hugged Annie crying as he held her.

"Stop it now John. Knowing what you know now would you have done things differently?"

"No way." said John excitedly, "I will always love you. I would do it all over again."

"That is the way I feel also, so Johnny, feel happy for me." They, wanting to make Annie's last hour as she had asked, started to reminisce all the high points in the twenty-seven years they had together. It was after one the next morning that Annie drifted off to sleep. John and Sarah stayed with her that night until late that morning, but she never awoke again. It was two days later that Annie's heart stopped beating. From that moment on John was in a fog. He barely remembered the funeral. Step by step they walked, scattering leaves and trampling the grass. Under measured and heavy steps, they approached the grave site. The minister's words still echoing in John's mind when he left the site. He heard the workmen moving toward the site preparing to cover the casket of his beloved Annie. Death had torn his life apart, leaving only memories, tears and loneliness. He didn't even remember that his only sibling, his sister was there.

It was about two weeks later that he came out of his fog and realized that his daughter was taking care of him. She was cooking for him, washing his clothes, and keeping house clean for him.

"Dad, come up and have something to eat." John was sitting in the family room. It was six steps up to the kitchen from the family room. There was a railing that divided the two rooms. "Come on Dad," Sarah continued, "you have to eat. You can't live long on the scraps you've been eating."

"That's all right," said John tearfully, "I will be with your mother. I don't have any reason to live any longer."

"Come on Dad. You have me to live for, not forgetting that God has a reason for you being here. Live for God. Now stop this foolishness and come up and eat."

"I'm not hungry."

"I am not asking you to eat for pleasure, I'm asking you to eat for necessity."

"Later," responded John."

"Now," said Sarah sternly. "I have some soup and fruit for you. It will get cold." John seeing that Sarah was getting upset went up and sat at the kitchen table. Sarah said grace and John started to eat his soup.

"I don't know how to thank you," started John, becoming aware of all that his daughter was doing for him. "I don't know what I would have done without you."

"Stop that," she responded. "You took care of me for about twenty-six years. I have been here for three weeks. Which reminds me, Dad, I've been away from my office all this time. I need to get back or I will lose my patients. But, Dad, I can't leave you until I know you can take care of yourself."

"Honey, I've always been able to take care of myself. I just have to grieve a while. Why don't you go home? I'll be all right. I don't want you to lose your job. I'll always be grateful for your support and care you have given me. I don't know what I would have done without you. I will just grieve a little. I then will move on. I promise."

"Are you sure Dad? Just say the word and I will stay as long as is necessary. I'm a doctor. I can get work anywhere. You know that I'm looking to come back to Ohio. I'm just looking for the right deal."

"I appreciate all that you have done and I appreciate your offer. But, honey, I have to learn to move on by myself. I admit that I've been in a fog up to now, but I'm back to being myself again. Like I said, I have to grieve by myself."

"All right Dad if you're sure you will be OK, I'll call for a flight back to California tomorrow."

"Don't worry about me. I also have Bill and Sally next door. They are like family to me."

"Yes I know," said Sarah. "They have been here every day since the funeral. It was really wonderful of them to bring so much food these past days. I think that from here on however you will have to cook for yourself."

"It's a good thing that Annie taught me and let me cook some of the time. To tell you the truth, which I'm sure you already know, your mom didn't do a good job at cooking steaks or fish. She over cooked them. She felt a little more is always better."

"I know Dad and don't think I didn't appreciate that."

"Well, I just wanted you to know. I can take care of myself." It was two days later when it was time for Sarah to leave. After breakfast, John drove her to the airport. They said their goodbyes in tears and soon John was on his way home. It was on the way home that he realized how much he was going to miss Sarah. He skipped lunch and had a sandwich for dinner. This he repeated for several weeks. His neighbors invited him often but he found excuses and didn't attend. One day his neighbors Bill and Sally showed up at his door. Sally was carrying several covered dishes and so was Bill.

"You won't come to us, so we decided to come to you," said Sally and went directly to the kitchen.

"You guys are something else," said John in a state of shock. "You are both so sweet, but you shouldn't have," he said feeling grateful for their thoughtfulness. "I'm sorry that I've put you off, but I haven't felt that well."

"No wonder," said Bill. "Look at you. You must have lost ten or more pounds. Well, we are going to fatten you up to your normal weight."

"Johnny," said Sally getting more serious. "You are stronger than this. Of course you are going to miss Annie. We miss her too. What do you think that Annie is feeling seeing you like this?"

"I'm fine; I just have to grieve a little. I promise that I will move on. I just don't know yet where to move on to."

"What does your daughter Sarah say to you about your depression like behavior?" asked Sally.

"She calls me every day," said John. "You know, there is three hours difference between here and California. She calls when she gets off of work at about five her time. That is about eight here. I tell her that everything is fine."

"You say that you don't have anything to move on to," said Bill. "What about your writing? I remember that you were working on a new novel."

"I just don't feel like writing. The truth is that I can't think of anything to write. I'm just not in the mood. Besides, I always wrote for Annie's future. I don't have that goal anymore."

"You also had a hobby painting pictures of places you have been. I think you have a big talent there." said Bill. "What happened to that interest?"

"Right now my mind is just a blank. I just want to work around the house. Thinking is kind of painful to me."

"I know what you need," said Sally as if a wonderful idea came to her suddenly. "You need two things. First you need to have something that keeps you busy for a while. Secondly you need to see people that are worse off then you are. Knowing you, I'm sure you will want to help them."

"What are you talking about?" asked John.

"Well you know that the medical office I work at closes every Wednesday," answered Sally. "I chose to spend that time for charity work. Sometimes I go to the soup kitchen down town. They can use all the help they can get. Why don't you come with me next Wednesday? You can talk to Mr. Perkins who runs the place. You can just watch for a while. Knowing you and your kindness and generosity I know that you will not want to just watch. Whatever you do is OK. What do you say?"

"I don't think so," responded John. "I wouldn't be any good the way I feel."

"That is a lot of boloney," said Sally. "I know you better than you do. You need some distraction. I'll come around next Wednesday. Let's go at lunch time. There will be less people there at that time. You can just see what it's like. If it's not your thing then you can leave a donation. They can always use money. Remember they have to buy the food they serve."

"Don't they get any food donation?" asked John.

"Of course they do, but it is never enough."

"I think it is a great idea," said Bill, who had been keeping silent till now. "I would go with you if I didn't have to work Wednesday. If you decide to go on a Saturday I will go with you. It's a great opportunity to see how the other side of the city works."

"I'll think about it," said John wanting to close the conversation on the subject. "What is going on in the world of science?"

"Never mind science," said Sally. "Dinner is ready on the table. I'm hungry. Let's eat."

"I'm not hungry," said John sadly.

"When you taste my food, you will get hungry," assured Sally jokingly.

"How can I argue with that?" said John with a weak smile. After they finished eating Sally noticed that John had eaten a good share of the food. She decided not to say anything. This is not the time, she thought, to be funny. After cleaning the kitchen they sat and talked about how their other friends were getting along. Soon Sally and Bill decided that it was time to go home. John wouldn't stop thanking them for their generosity and friendship. John promised that he wouldn't make them bring the food to him again. They packed up their utilities and each hugging John and left. John watched TV for awhile and then went to bed.

It was about two days later that John received an invitation from Bill and Sally to dinner. This time John didn't refuse. Although Bill and Sally tried to stay away from bring up Annie, John kept bring up how much he missed her. How everything he tried to do reminded him of her.

"Tomorrow is Wednesday," said Sally "You are going with me to the soup kitchen right?"

"I don't think so," responded John. "What I was thinking, since you guy have supplied me dinner so many times, is that it is my turn. So I was thinking about my taking you guy out to dinner."

"Thank you, but some other time," said Sally. "Tomorrow you and I are going to the soup kitchen.

"Yes and I have a previous engagement with a client," added Bill. "So I can't make it. I always make this type of commitment on Wednesday since Sally always goes to the kitchen."

"Besides," added Sally. "I need your company. I don't like to go alone."

"Ouch," said John.

"What's the matter," asked Sally worried over John's pain.

"It hurts when you twist my arm to get your way," said John with a big smile.

"You're back to your old self," said Sally. "Does that mean that you are going?"

"No, it just means that you are twisting my arms and it's uncomfortable."

"Please John," begged Sally. "Do it for me."

"We will see," he answered.

The next morning about ten thirty Sally came knocking on the door.

"Are you ready?" she asked.

"You are persistent," answered John. He was all dressed and ready to go. He knew her well enough to know that she would be there in the morning.

"Don't you know yet that Bill and I care very much for you?"

"I know," answered John. "Let's go and get this over with." It only took about twenty minutes to get there. They were met at the door with a kind looking gentleman. Sally had apparently called ahead.

"Good morning," he said. "You must be John Cane. I'm Tom Perkins. I have the honor and the responsibility of running this place."

"Good morning," said John. "I'm so glad to meet you. Sally has told me so much about what you have accomplished here."

"She exaggerates a lot" he responded. Then, he turns to Sally, "How are you Sally. I would like to show John around. Do you want to go with us?"

"No, you go ahead. I know what has to be done before the noon crowd comes in." Tom showed John the kitchen, the ovens, the food storage area and the food distribution counter which faced the dining area where they first entered the facility. He then took him upstairs via the inside entrance. He had to use a key to open the door.

"We keep this door locked to keep the tenants upstairs from coming down and raiding the kitchen. They have an outside entrance that is also locked. Each tenant has a key. They are told if they let anyone else in they will lose their key"

"I can see how that could cause a problem," said John

"There are two rooms up here for the homeless. There is one room for the men with ten beds, and one room for the women with ten beds." explained Tom. When they went back into the dining room John noticed that some people were starting to come in. Sally was at the counter dishing out food. Each person would grab a tray and as they passed by Sally would place a bowl of soup on each tray. Another young lady would place two slices of bread on the tray and another would place what looked like to John, a slice of ham.

"If I decided to help here what would you have me doing?" asked John.

"You could be cooking, dishing out food at the counter or to start until you get used to the place just cleaning the tables. We have fifteen tables to keep clean. You could also be washing dishes. And if we have more help then we need you could be going to a warehouse or food distributer who is willing to get rid of food that he is stuck with at his costs or less. Since this is a voluntary service you can just sit here and talk to the people. I understand that you are an author. Maybe you can get information for your next book. It doesn't matter. I know from past experience that after you talk to a few people you will want to do more."

"What days are you most short of help?" asked John getting interested.

"We can use help most days," answered Tom. "However, Mondays and Thursdays are probably the worst days for help. We could always use help on the weekends. We always need someone to pick up something. Drivers are probably the biggest shortage we have. But don't worry about that for now. Just come. You'll find something to do."

John went to the soup kitchen Monday at about eleven as he had done with Sally the Wednesday before. Tom introduced John to the two other helpers, Martha and Betty. At first he cleaned the tables and washed dishes. He kept busy during the noon hour and helped until to his surprise it was near diner time. After the people finished eating he helped with clearing the tables, washing them and later washing the dishes. He started going to the facility several days the following week. At first he just cleaned the tables and washed the dishes. He did get to talk with some of the street people who came to eat there. He was impressed with some of their stories. Most spent the day hours looking for work. Tom also helped them, telling of places that might be looking for laborers. After several weeks, Tom let John serve at the food counter when they were short of servers. John began to feel at home. Several times he made trips to get food. He once made a trip to Amish country for chickens and other meats that were donated or sold at a reasonable price. Several times John paid for it from his own pocket and refused to get reimbursed. Later Tom, after learning that John did a lot of cooking at home, let John come up with several different receipt that were tasty and reasonable in cost. In those cases John did the cooking. It was near the end of October when John got interested in a young woman and a child that started to come in for evening meals. John thought that the woman was probably in her early twenties and the child was in her early teens or about twelve. He felt that they were too young to be street people. For several days he would smile at them and wish them a good evening. Finally one evening he stopped to talk with them.

"Do you want to tell me about your problems?" asked John. "Perhaps I could help."

"No thank you," said the woman.

"Grace is very depressed," said the younger girl. My name is Amy. Grace doesn't talk too much."

"Do you two live together?" asked John. "Do you have a home to live in?"

"It is home to us," said Grace. "Why do you care?" she said sounding unfriendly.

"I just wondered if I could help" said John and left to let them finish their meal.

For the next few days that he saw them he would just say hello, calling them by name. He felt that if they got to see him often and that he would addressed them on a personal bases, that they would loosen up a bit. It was a little over a week to Thanksgiving that John saw them again. John had stopped coming to the soup kitchen as often becoming interested in writing again. Tom said that he understood and was grateful for the help he had given. He told John that he could come whenever he found time or wanted a rest from his writing. What attracted John this day was that he saw Grace fighting back tears.

"What is the matter?" he asked, seeing the wet eyes.

"Nothing," said Grace starting to tears up more.

"Some bully stole our blankets," said Amy. "I had a blanket that I brought with me and Grace had one and this big guy stole them and our pillow."

"Well where was this at?" asked John.

"We have a box we live in behind the restaurant down town. Grace found the box in front of a house near the restaurant. That is where we met. I helped her bring the box to where it is now. With our blankets and the pillow that an old man gave us we were very comfortable."

"I don't think we have the box anymore," said Grace. "I saw one of the bullies watching for us to leave. I think they were going to move in. Why is God punishing us? What have we done?"

"The restaurant owner used to bring leftover food to Grace and me and two old men that also lived back there. Now because of these hoodlums he doesn't bring anything out anymore. That is why we started to come here," Explained Amy.

"So where are you going to sleep tonight?" asked John being deeply concerned.

"I don't know," said Grace.

"You can't sleep outside tonight," said John. "The weatherman said that it was going to go below freezing tonight."

"We asked Tom if it was possible for us to stay here but he said that his beds are full. He said he even has old men and woman sleeping on the floor between the bunks," said Grace. "Why has God forgotten us?"

"He hasn't forgotten you," said John making up his mind as what he had to do. "You two are coming with me tonight. I am a widower. I live alone and have a house with five bedrooms."

"We can't do that," said Grace sternly.

"Why not?" asked John.

"You are a perfect stranger," said Grace. "We don't know you."

"First of all, I'm not perfect and I'm not a stranger. You have known me for some time now. I've been feeding you for some time. Anyway, my name is John Cane. Now you know me. Besides, don't you believe that God has sent me? He might have been testing you. I am a born again Christian. You have nothing to be afraid of except freezing to death tonight."

"I don't know what to do," said Grace seemingly to be relenting.

"Come on Grace," said Amy. "Do we have a choice?"

"God is giving you a hand," said John. "Do you really believe in God? What church do you belong to?"

"We go to the First Baptist Church," said Grace. "I'm a saved Christian and I'm trying to save Amy."

"That is great," said John. "Don't you see? We are brother and sisters in Christ."

"I don't know," said Grace. "Let us think about it." At that moment Tom came up to John.

John," he asked. "Can you wash the remainder dishes and close up? Martha had to leave early and I have a meeting I have to go to."

"Be glad too," said John. Then turning to Grace he added. "You two just stay here and think about it. Let me wash the dishes and I'll get back to you in a few minutes." John left them and went into the kitchen and washed the dishes. When he finished the dishes he found that Grace and Amy were gone. He felt a great pain in his stomach. He shut off all the light and went outside. As he was locking the door he heard a sound behind him. He turned. It was Amy.

"Is that offer still available?" she said. "I didn't want to leave Grace but I don't think I have a choice." Then seeing tears in John's eyes she questions him. "What is the matter? Are you all right?"

"I'm so glad to see you," said John. "Don't you know how much I care for you guys?"

"Does that include me?" asked Grace as she came around the corner of the building.

"Are you kidding," said John now tears clearly seen in the light of the store's night light. "I'm thrilled to see both of you. I had given up hope that I would ever see you too again."

"Why do you care so much about two strange girls you don't even know?" asked Grace. "You act like you love us like your own daughters. Why?"

"Oh Grace," said John. "Don't you know that God is love? We are all children under him. He has put love in my heart for you two. You are like my children. Why else would I be so concern for your safety?"

"Take us home daddy," said Grace trying to be funny and also keep from crying herself. John led them to his car and twenty minutes later he pulled into his garage. He then took them upstairs to the last two rooms down the hallway.

"You can each have your own rooms or sleep together if you like. It is your choice."

"I would like to sleep with you, Grace," said Amy. "Is that acceptable with you Grace?"

"Yes," she said. "I think for awhile that will make us feel safer."

So be it," said John. "However, before you slide you dirty bodies under the clean sheets you need to wash up. Wait here for a minute and let me get you something to wear while I wash your clothes." He then went through his closets and came up with night wear for each.

"Grace this is my wife's evening gown. I'm sure it will fit. Amy, All I have for you is the long shirt that I think will cover you pretty well. So now go into the bathroom one at a time and take a shower. Throw out your clothes so I can wash them."

"I have one request," said Grace. "I want to wash the clothes. Just show me where the washer and drier are and I want to do the washing. I can at least do that."

"As you wish," said John. He then took her down stairs and showed her the laundry room. "I'm going to the family room and watch the late news. You do your thing and then go to bed. I will see you in the morning. We will do the talking then. Good night girls."

The next morning John woke up early, worrying about the girls. He wondered if Sally had any idea what she had gotten John into. He had to admit that it did snap him out of his depression. He had seen Bill and Sally several times since he started at the soup kitchen. He had talked to his daughter every day since, however he had not told her anything about his time at the kitchen. John made breakfast of eggs, hash browns, and breakfast sausage. About nine, he decided to call the girls,

"Girls, it's time to get up, breakfast is ready."

"We are up," said Grace. "We are still in the night clothes you gave us. I didn't go down and do the washing. I was too tired."

"That's all right," said John. "Come down and eat before it gets cold. You can wash later. You have all day." The girls came down a few minutes later. Grace was in Annie's house coat, and Amy was in John extra long shirt. It fit Amy like a dress. They each sat at the table where there was a dish with breakfast. After they had settled in, John said grace. "Now girls, while you are eating, is a good time for each of you to tell me your story. I need to know so that I can see if I can help in some way. Grace let's start with you."

"I don't know where to start," she answered.

"Tell me about your parents first," said John trying to get her started.

"Well both of my parents have died. My father died of a heart attack when I was fifteen. My mother lived to see me get married. I had a brother but he was killed in the service. He was much older than I. I was a late arrival. My mother was over fifty when she had me. She died about two years ago. I have no other family."

"Tell me about your husband," said John trying to get her to talk more openly.

"I met my husband at work. We worked for IDC, which stands for Industrial Designers Company. Ralph was the Financial Officer and I was his assistant. You see after my first years in college I started to study biology. I wanted to be a nurse. When my mother got sick I couldn't continue. I had studied finance in the first years of college so I applied for the assistant job."

"Well with all that education, how did you end up in the street?" asked John being puzzled by what he was hearing.

"You don't really want to know," said Grace. "It's a long story."

"Well give me a short version."

"Ralph and I got married and after mother died we took my inheritance and all our savings and put it all down on a house. We bought just a few pieces of used furniture and a new bed and move in. We were very happy for a little over a year. Then Ralph came down with lung cancer. He didn't even smoke. I took him to the Cancer Center in Chicago. They couldn't help him. It took all the money we had and he still died."

"Oh Grace, I'm so sorry," said John. "What happened to your house?"

"Well at the same time, the company we worked for failed, and I was out of a job. Although I had missed so many days when I was in Chicago with Ralph, I would probably have been fired anyway. After I buried Ralph, I went looking for a job. One day I came home and found a strange bracket and a lock on my front door. I went around the back and found that it had the same contraption on it. As I came back to the front of the house I saw a tow truck starting to tow my car away. When I tried to stop him he told me that the car was being repossessed. So I was left in the cold. I lost everything."

"I'll try to change all that," promised John. "Give me the address of your home and the bank that held your mortgage." After Grace gave him all the information he asked for, John got a big smile on his face. "That is great. That is the same bank that I have half of my money in. That gives me a great advantage. How much was the house and how much was your equity in it?"

"We paid about One hundred sixty thousand. We put down one hundred thousand and then put anything that we had left at the end of each month into it above the required monthly payment. We wanted to pay off the mortgage as soon as possible."

"That is a miscarriage of justice," said John getting angry. "Let me see what I can do about that."

"Do you think you can do something," asked Grace.

"At least I should be able to let you get some of your clothes." said John. "Is there anything else that you would want?"

"It would be nice to get my car," said Grace.

"I thought that your car got repossessed?"

"My car got repossessed but my husband's car is in the garage"

"Won't that car be repossessed if it is out in the street?" asked John.

"No it is fully paid," answered Grace. "When Ralph got sick he got a lawyer to transfer everything we owned into my name. He also recommended that we had at least one car fully paid."

"OK then," said John feeling that he had all the information he needed. "Now Amy, it's your turn. Tell me your story."

"I don't have much to tell," answered Amy. "I was in school when a police man came and got me. He told me that my parents were killed in an auto accident."

"What did your parents do as a living?"

"They were investigators for a brokerage company. They investigated company's financial health I think."

"How did you get on the street with Grace?"

"My parent's lawyer, I don't remember his name, got me and placed me in a small orphanage in Cincinnati. It was terrible. They had a Miss Seaton run the place. She had a thing for a boy named George. He had his way with all the girls and Miss Seaton didn't care. He tried to take my clothes off and I kicked and fought him. Since I wouldn't give in to him he beat me up. When I told Miss Seaton she punished me for not getting along with the other kids. She sent me to the bedroom without supper. I packed my backpack and took a blanket from the bed and using a bed sheet I lowered myself down from the second story and ran away."

"How did you get back to this area?" asked John.

"I hitched a ride with a truck that was going to Cleveland. He dropped me off down town."

"How did you meet Grace?"

"I was walking back from down town to see if I could sneak into my home," answered Amy, "when I saw Grace trying to drag a big box down the street."

"I had gone to the restaurant to see if I could get something to eat." interrupted Grace. "I heard that they threw away leftovers in the trash. I found that a couple of old men were sleeping there in cardboard boxes. So I went looking for a box and as luck had it I found a large box on the curb by a house on a side street. I think it was a refrigerator box. It was made of cardboard with a wooden frame. We took it and set it between the kitchen wall which protruded out from the rest of the building, and the trash bin that was against the rear wall. At the end of the day the owner would bring out leftover food in dishes and asked that we would leave the dishes on the door step when we finished. One day one of the old men said that a relative had found him and he was leaving with them. He gave me his blanket and pillow so Amy and I both had a blanket and we slept comfortably at night in the box."

"That's when the two bad men came back there," continued Amy. "They were such brats. They wouldn't bring the dishes back so the owner stopped bringing out food. That's when we heard about the soup kitchen and started to go there."

"We were all right there," said Grace, "until they decided to take our box and our blankets. You know the rest."

"Amy, what is your home address?" asked John. Amy gave John her address and street name. "You lived on Kenridge Drive? That's right here in Fairlawn. Well that is great," said John. "I have to go out now for a little while. You girls wash your clothes, get dressed and if I'm not home by noon help yourselves to lunch."

CHAPTER TWO

Unexpected Success

IT ONLY TOOK JOHN A few minutes to get to the bank. On the right, inside the bank, was a row of offices. John looked into the first office. A young lady was on the phone. John stood in the door way and waited until she got off the phone.

"May I help you?" she asked.

"Yes, I would like to talk to someone on paying off a house mortgage."

"That would be Mr. Norton," she said. "His office is the last one near the rear door." John walked to the last office and found that the man in the office was talking with another person.

"Take a seat out there," he said. "I'll be with you in just a few minutes." A few feet from the office was a table with four soft lounge type chairs. John grabbed one and sat down. It was about eleven when John got there. It was near twelve when Mr. Norton finished with his client.

"What can I do for you?" he asked then continued without waiting for an answer. "It is noon and I'd like to go to lunch. Make it short."

"I would like to pay off a house mortgage for a friend of mine," said John.

"Who is the owner and what is the house address?"

"Her name is Grace Perry," said John and her address is,"

"I know about that," said Mr. Norton. "We repossessed that house almost a month ago. She hadn't paid us for over three months. The house is now the property of this bank. We have a buyer that is interested in the property. It is too late."

"I can't believe that," said John. "She has paid more than one hundred thousand on the property. She only owes about forty thousand. Would you cheat her out of that equity?"

"We sell the property for whatever we can get. The goal is to get our money back. If there is anything left we will give it to her. Now, I'm sorry but I have a lunch date."

"Can't you even let her in to get some of her clothes?"

"I'm sorry, everything belongs to the bank." With John standing there he left. John drove home as fast as he could and walked into his office without seeing the girls and immediately called the main office in Pittsburg PA. A woman answered to phone.

"How may I help you?" she asked.

"I have a problem with one of your branches. I would like to talk with one who has authority over the branches."

"That would be Mr. Arnold," she said. "Please hold on and let me see if he is in." This to John sounded like a typical excuse. He was surprised when a man answered the phone.

"This is Burt Arnold. How may I help you," he asked. John decided to start at the beginning.

"Very good friends of mine bought a house in Akron. The house was purchased for around one hundred sixty thousand dollars. They put down one hundred thousand, got a mortgage for the remainder and paid each month double the monthly payment required, wanting to pay off the mortgage as quickly as they could. As fortune would have it the husband came down with lung cancer. After many doctors she took him to the cancer center in Chicago. At the same time the company she worked for went under. After her husband died and was buried she went looking for a job so she could pay up the dept that had accumulated."

"So, how can I help you?" asked Mr. Arnold apparently being puzzled.

"I'm getting to that," said John. "When she got home one day she found that her house had been padlock front and back. She couldn't get her clothes, any money that she had inside, and she couldn't get into the garage to get her car. She was left in the street without even a blanket. My name is John Cane. I am a writer. I have friends in the newspaper business. My first reaction was to withdraw my money from your bank, which amounts to around a half million, and call my friends in the news paper. They would have a field day with this information. However, I've cooled down and decided to handle this in a friendly way. So I went to the bank which held the mortgage, which incidentally happened to be my bank, and hers. I saw a Mr. Norton. He said that the bank owned the house and it was too late. I offered to pay the complete mortgage, all interest accumulated as well as any penalty for paying ahead of time"

"I'm glad you did," said Mr. Arnold. "By the way are you Johnny Cane, the author of The Top Of The Hill, and Adventures of Tom Corrie, and a few others I can't name right now?"

"Guilty" said John. "He wouldn't even consider letting her in to get some of her clothes. He said everything belonged to the bank."

"That's not true if the equity of the house is more than the mortgage," said Mr. Arnold. "Listen; let me have a couple of hours to review this case. I will at least promise to let her in to get some of her possessions."

"Will you call me?" asked John.

No, I will take care of this first and then go to lunch. I have other things I have to take care of. Just go back to the branch around two this afternoon and they will have everything ready for you. Have a great day," he ended and hung up."

When John came out of his office he called the girls to come down stairs. They were in the upstairs T.V. room. The girls had washed their clothes got dressed and came down looking like they were ready to go out.

"Girls have you had lunch yet?" he asked.

"No," said Amy, "We were waiting for you. Where have you been?"

"I was down here in my office," said John. "I was on the phone. Let's eat. I have to go out to the bank around two."

"Any luck on my house?" asked Grace.

"I think that I can get inside so you can get your clothes and your car. I'll know for sure at two o'clock this afternoon." After lunch, John prepared a list of argument he intended to present to Mr. Norton. He was going to go down fighting. He was not confident that Mr. Arnold in Pittsburg was going to help that much. At about one-forty-five he put on his coat and prepared to leave.

"Good luck" said Amy. "I wonder, will it be possible for you to go to my house and get me a coat?"I would like the ability to go out with you and Grace if you go to Grace's house."

"Let's see what I can do for Grace first," said John. "If it comes to that, I can always find you a jacket of mine that would fit you. For that matter, why don't you go through my closet while I'm gone? I have many jackets in the guest closet. Some are already too small for me."

"We will watch some TV while you're out," said Grace. "I don't think I can do anything else except pray."

"Praying is a great idea," said John as he left.

When John got to the bank he went directly to the last office which was Mr. Norton's office. The office was empty. He back tracked to the office just before Mr. Norton's office. He had seen a young lady in it as he walked passed it.

"Can you tell me, please," he asked. "Do you know where Mr. Norton is?"

"Mr. Norton is out for the day," she answered him. "Can I be of help to you?"

"I was talking to him about paying off a mortgage," said John getting a bit upset.

"I'm sorry, but I can't help you there," she answered. John was now very angry. He started to walk out of the bank when he heard his name from someone behind him.

"Mr. Cane?" she repeated as John turned around.

"Yes, that's me," said John.

"My name is Betty Belden. I'm the assistant bank manager. I will take care of you. Please follow me to my office." John followed her to her office. The walk caused John's anger to subside somewhat. Her office was bigger than Mr. Norton's office. It was more elegant."Please have a seat."

"Are you familiar with my request?" asked John not knowing why they had enlisted a higher bank officer to handle him. That concerned him.

"Yes," she answered very sweetly. "I spoke with Mr. Arnold. Everything is taken care of." She then pulled out a large envelope and pulled out a key. *Well,* thought John, *they were at least going to let him in the house.* "When you use the key on the bank's lock you will be able to remove the brackets. Return them to the bank at your earliest convenience." She then pushed a sheet of paper toward John. "The total of the mortgage, interest, taxes, and other minor cost is forty-eight thousand six hundred and forty-five dollars. How are you going to pay for this?" John was shocked. He never expected this. He was not prepared.

"Can you take $50,000 from my Money Market account and put it into my checking account?" asked John.

"Yes," said Betty. "I can do that right here on my computer." It took only a couple of minutes. "Now, if you will sign this transfer and write out your check to this branch, I will give you the other documents." John was in a state of shock. Did he understand what was going on? As the realization worked up in his system his stomach began to have strange feelings. The joy he felt was greater than he had experienced for years. He couldn't remember when he felt so great. He quickly took out his check book and wrote out the check. Upon receiving the check, she pulled out the papers from the envelope and pushed one toward him. "This is the receipt for your check. Please sign it and return a copy to me." She then pulled out a darker sheet. It was the mortgage agreement. She stamped it with large black letters that read, 'Paid in Full.' The other sheet in the envelope was the deed to the property. She put everything back in the envelope and handed it to John. "I want you to understand that the house has been winterized."

"Which means?" asked John.

"It means that there is no electricity, no gas no water. The pipes have been drained to keep them from freezing. I think that takes care of anything," she said. "Can I help you with anything else?"

"No," responded John as if he were in a hypnotic trance, "I think that handles everything just fine. Thank you very much for your time and effort. I am well pleased."

"Thank you for your business and patience. You have a nice day now."

"Thank you," responded John as he got up and started to walk out. As he walked out the bank he felt like his feet hardly touched the ground. He got so much more than he had expected. He got home and immediately called the girls who were watching T.V. in the upstairs T.V. room. They came down immediately upon hearing him call.

"Girls I want you to sit at the kitchen table," said John. "We have something important to discuss." The girls obeyed without question. They knew what the subject was about. They didn't want to hold up the details by asking dumb questions. John put the envelope on the table and pulled out the key that Ms. Belden had given him.

Oh great," said Grace. "Then we can get into the house? Let's go right now."

"Not so fast," said John. "We are not finished yet. First the house is winterized. There is no electricity, no gas and no water. Besides, I think you want to see these documents first." John then pulled out the mortgage paper and handed it to Grace. Grace's eyes opened wide not believing what she saw. Then John pulled out the deed and gave it to her. Now the surprise turned to tears. She got up and threw her arms around John's neck. She then saw the receipt.

"You paid off my mortgage?" she asked through her tears. "You are something so special. The house is entirely mine?"

"Of course it is all yours," said John. "However, we have to talk. What are your desires for your house?"

"Please don't think I'm not grateful, but I would like to be independent and move into my own house."

"I don't think you should consider moving in yet. I would like you to stay here. First, since you house is without utilities the cost of maintaining the house is low. You only need to pay the real estate tax. I think you should stay here until you get a job and save a little."

"I know you are right but I hate to be a burden on you," said Grace with affection in her voice.

"Honey, you are not a burden on me. I am a lonely widower with only one daughter and she is in California. I would love two daughters that keep me company."

"Then can we call you Daddy," asked Amy.

"I would love that," said John with tears showing in his eyes.

"Why shouldn't we call you father?" said Grace. "We love you like a father besides you are doing what my father would have done if he were alive."

"That is so sweet," said John. "But we should go to the house and get some of your clothes and other thing you may want."

"I want to go too," said Amy.

"Have you a coat to wear?"

"Yes," said Amy happily, "I found a zipper type jacket that fit me perfectly." They all got their coats and left for Grace's house. John brought his tool box. When they got there John asked the girls to stay in the warm auto until he removed the lock and brackets on the front door. That done the girls went inside to pack while John removed the rear lock and hardware. Grace only took about fifteen minutes to pack the clothes she wanted. Her finger got too cold to do any more packing. They left and were home by four o'clock. Grace drove her own car home back to John's house. John's garage had plenty of room for two cars.

"I see what you mean," said Grace. "It was colder inside then it is outside." They were all happy to be back to John's house. John went down to the freezer and brought up some chicken legs and thighs.

"Let me do the cooking," said Grace. "I'm a pretty good cook. Besides I want to pull my weight around here."

"Do you really want to do the cooking?" asked John. "You don't have to try to balance or repay what I've done for you."

"I know, Daddy," said Grace. "I couldn't ever repay you so I'm not even going to try." She saw John smiling and asked. "Why are you smiling? Don't you think I can cook?"

"No I'm smiling because you called me Daddy."

"I wasn't just talking what I said before. You are more of a father then most kids have. Does it bother you?"

"No," said John. "I love it. Go cook us a special dinner." She did and it was better than John and Amy had imagined. After dinner they sat drinking coffee and discussing the changes that had occurred in their lives.

"Amy," asked John. "Do you have a key to your house?"

"No," said Amy. "But I know where my mother hid a key. There is a false rock in our yard that opens and she usually hides a key inside. I don't know if it's still there. I don't know why it shouldn't be."

"First thing tomorrow morning we will go to your house and try to find out what has happened since your parents were killed. We will look for some documents. I would like to find out who the lawyer is on their case. It probably is also winterized so I don't think we should go now. We need our hands to recover from today's effort."

"Good," said Amy. "I could use some of my clothes to."

The next morning John was up at seven. He decided to return to his normal routine. He had not done this since Annie died. After dressing and shaving he went down and got on the treadmill. A half hour later he went to his office and read the bible. It was about eight-forty-five when he would go to the kitchen to cook breakfast. This was his normal routine. Annie would show up about nine and they would eat together. This time it was different. He heard the T.V. upstairs. Amy had gotten up early and was waiting for him. John realized that he had to change his routine.

"Amy," he yelled at the stairway. "Are you up?"

"Yes, Grace and I are up," said Amy. "We came downstairs and heard you on the treadmill. So we came up here to wait for you."

"Well come down and have breakfast," said John. After they ate John went up, took a shower, and was ready to travel at ten fifteen. The girls were ready with their coats in their hands. A few minutes later they were at Amy's house. The key was where Amy thought it would be. The house was very elegant. It was a ranch type house with three bedrooms. On the left were the living room, the dining room and the kitchen. Off the kitchen was an elegant family room. On the right were the three bedrooms. The smallest room was the one closest to the front of the house. Amy's Father had that set up as his office.

"What are we looking for?" asked Amy. "I mean besides my clothes."

"I am looking for any valuable documents," said John, "like mortgage, last will, and documents like that."

"I know that dad had a metal box with a key lock on it," said Amy.

"Do you know where that is?" asked John.

"I think he kept it in the safe," answered Amy. "I think it's in the closet." John went to the closet. Inside he found a short file cabinet. On the left it had a small drawer on top and two filing drawers under it. On the right was a door with a lock. John went through the file drawers and found nothing that could help.

"Do you know where the key is to the cabinet door?" asked John.

"I don't know," said Amy. "Maybe it is in the desk."

"What can I do to help?" said Grace feeling useless.

"Honey, wait until we solve this problem, and then you can help Amy in choosing the clothes to pack." John then went to the desk. In the main drawer he found a little box with keys in it. All the key rings had a label on it except one set of two keys. John guessed that one of those keys would open the door on the file cabinet. He was right. Inside he found a safe with a combination lock. Below the safe were two shelves. There was nothing there that could help.

"Amy, do you know the combination of the safe?" asked John.

"I don't know it," said Amy.

"Do you have any idea where it would be?"

"I have no idea," she answered.

"Everything we want is probably in that safe," said John. "We have to get in there."

"There are tools in the basement," added Amy. "I'm sure there is a drill."

"Before we do that we should try to find the combination," said John almost to himself. "Wait a minute. I remember reading a novel where the owner of a safe stuck the combination on the bottom of a desk drawer." John went to the desk and removed each drawer one at a time. There was no combination under any of them. "There is only one drawer that it could be under; the drawer in the file cabinet." He pulled the drawer out as far as it would go. Then getting on his hands and knees he looked under the drawer. "Bingo," he said out load. Taped under the drawer was a yellow tag with the combination stamped on it. John soon had the safe open. There among other things he found the metal box. He brought it out and set in on the desk. "I hope the other key on the key ring fits this box. It did, and John opened the box. Inside he found what he was looking for. There was a deed to the house.

"What is that?" asked Amy.

"It is the deed to your house. That proves that the house has no mortgage. That is great. No one except the tax man can foreclose on your house."

"What are the other papers," asked Grace who was eager to help.

"The important one is this one," said John holding up a document. It is Amy's parent's last will and testament. It shows that in case of both parents death that all their possessions go to Amy."

"What do we do now?" asked Amy.

"The important information on this document is the lawyer's name. It is Bruce Walton. You and Grace go into your bed room and start packing. We got to get out of here before we freeze. I'm going out in the car where it is warmer and call the lawyer." A few minutes later, sitting in the car, John reached Mr. Walton.

"Mr. Walton," started John. "My name is John Cane. I'm calling in regards to Amy Findel."

"Have you found her?" he asked showing great concern.

"She is staying with me," said John. "I would like to talk with you with regards to her house and other property she has inherited."

"I'm eager to speak with you also," he answered. "Is she all right? She escaped from the orphanage and I've been looking for her for months. I will have time at three this afternoon. Can you be here?"

"Yes we will be there," assured John.

"Please bring Amy with you."

"Of course, we will both be in your office at three." Bruce gave John his office address and phone number and hung up. Five minutes later Grace and Amy showed up carrying two suit cases.

"You plan on staying awhile," said John in humor.

"I couldn't decide on what I wanted," said Amy. "Besides you said that you would adopt me."

"That is a great idea. Let ask the lawyer to set it up. We have an appointment at three this afternoon."

"How about me?" asked Grace with a smile on her face.

"I would love to have two more daughters," said John being more serious than the girls expected.

After lunch they sat down and talked about the future. They clearly had three houses all together.

"You have five options,' started John. "My favorite is that you both sell your homes and stay with me as my daughters. A second option is for each to go and live in your own home. I don't like this one at all. A third option is to sell Amy's home and you both move to Grace's home. A fourth option is to sell Grace's home and with the money Grace would buy Amy's home. Then you both could live together there. A fifth option is to sell Amy's home and Grace moves into her own home and Amy stays here with me. Understand that nothing will take place until Grace gets a job. You girls think this over and we will talk about it later after Grace finds work.

"Amy and I will talk about it together," said Grace. "In the mean time I would rather not go with you to the lawyer. I would like to go to an employment agency to get a job. I wouldn't be of any help to you anyway."

"You are always a help to us," said John. "However I understand your concerns. Go do your thing." A few minutes later after making a few phone calls, Grace took her car and left. Around two-thirty John and Amy went to the lawyer's office.

"Hi," said Bruce. "You must be John Cane. And you are Amy," he said pointing to Amy. "You don't know the trouble I've had because of you. I have taken care of your house, paid your bills to keep you from losing it, and have processed the will so that everything is now in your name."

"Thank you so much," said Amy. "I'm sorry to cause you any problems."

"That's OK, Just as long as you are well. Why did you run away from the orphanage?" Between John and Amy they related the whole story of how she was treated at the orphanage.

"That is terrible," he said at the end of their tale. I have to look into that. Right now I need a Guardian and executor."

"Well Mr. Walton, Amy has asked me to be her guardian and executor of her property," said John looking at Amy for approval. Amy smiled softly and shook her head up and down barely noticeable.

"That is great to hear. But please call me Bruce."

"Only if you call me John," responded John. "What I would like is for you to process the paper work for me to adopt Amy."

"I don't think that is a good idea right now. Processing for adoption can take months even years. Does your wife agree to the adoption?"

"No, I'm a widower. I'd be a single parent"

"That will make it even harder and take longer. Until that goes through I would have to send Amy back to child welfare. They would probable sent her back to an orphanage."

"I will not allow her to be sent anywhere. What do you suggest?"

"I think a faster way for her to stay with you is if you take her as a Foster Child. I can get that pretty quick. And she can stay with you until it goes through since I will assign you as the temporary guardian."

"Will you put through the papers for my adoption of Amy and also put in the papers for my adoption of Grace Perry?"

"Who now is Grace Perry?" asked Bruce.

"I met her when I met Amy. They were both on the street. I have helped her and she is now staying with me."

"I will need a lot more information on her," said Bruce.

"How much time do you have?" asked John feeling that he could put it off.

"I have as much time as it takes," he said. I also will need a financial statement from you." He hesitated for a few seconds and asked, "John Cane, are you the writer of a series of fictional novels?"

"Guilty," said John.

"Then that makes things easier. I will state that you intend to get a house keeper or governess if necessary. Money will be no problem. I will handle everything from here on. I will get the details on Grace later. I'll keep you informed. John gave Bruce his address and phone number and he and Amy left. On the way home Amy brought up the subject of the future.

"You know Dad," she started. "I have been thinking of the five options you said we had. I don't mean any disrespect. You know that I love you like my own true father. But I would like to live with Grace. She also likes my home more than hers. She is worried about a mortgage. She doesn't want to take on a new mortgage I told her no way would you let her take on a new mortgage. Besides if I live with her I would give her a big discount. So we will wait until she gets a job and then make a final decision. Anyway, whatever she decides, that is my thinking."

"That's fine sweetheart. You know you are a very smart young lady. You know that my only wish is to make you both happy, just as long as you don't forget me."

"I couldn't forget you even if I got amnesia. I would still think of you." When they got home Grace was just arriving behind them.

"Dad," she said. "I just couldn't get away sooner. I should have been here to make dinner. But the employment agency sent me to two interviews. I just got finished. I don't even know how I did. I didn't get any offers."

"It is after five," said John. "I can't believe how the time has flown. I'll tell you what, let's go out for dinner. We should celebrate our success. In only two days we have saved your house Grace, and got things settle with Amy's house. Let's celebrate."

"I have a desire for some fish, maybe some shrimp," said Amy.

"That sound great to me," said Grace.

"So be it," said John. "Let's go to Red Lobster." After dinner they were just entering the garage when they were hailed by Sally from next door. Grace recognized her immediately from her time at the soup kitchen.

"Hi Mrs. Stevens," said Grace. "I didn't know you lived next door."

"Hello young lady. I recognize you but I don't remember your name." Grace and Amy introduced themselves.

"It's so good to see you. What are you doing here?" John broke in and explained everything that had happen the last two days. He explained how he was working to adopt them.

"I just fell in love with these girls," he explained.

"That is so wonderful," said Sally. "You three have to come over to our house and have dinner with us and you can tell Bill and me all the details." After agreeing to go there the next evening they went into the house.

"You know," said John to the girls. "Sally makes the best meatloaf I have ever eaten. Hope she makes that tomorrow." A little while later the phone rang. It was John's daughter Sarah.

"Hi Dad," she said. "What is new with you?" John had not told her about Grace and Amy. He explained everything to her from the soup kitchen time to the present.

"So now," continued John, "I have asked the lawyer to prepare papers for me to adoption the two girls." Because Sarah hesitated for a few seconds John continued; "Do you have any objection or comments you want to make?"

"No," said Sarah. "I think it is so wonderful. It is more than I had hoped for. The girls will keep you occupied and I'd love a couple of baby sisters."

"Grace is twenty three. Not too much of a baby. I was just concern with your thoughts about the inheritance."

"That is silly," she said. "You are going to live another hundred years. I'm a pretty good doctor. I will have a pretty good nest egg of my own. I would love to have them listed on your will. I won't feel so alone in this world." They spoke a little longer and then Sarah said that she just got home from work and was getting hungry. After hanging up John explained to the girls everything that he had discussed with Sarah. He emphasized her delight at having two new sisters. Grace was still unconvinced.

"You know that I love you Dad," she said. "However, I feel that I would be stealing from Sarah. I don't even know her and yet I feel a love for her as my big sister. I don't want any hard feelings to come between us. Besides I don't deserve anything. You've done so much for me already. I don't even deserve that much."

"You have just given a great description of love, Grace," he answered.

CHAPTER THREE

The best of days

THE NEXT MORNING ABOUT NINE, after they had finished breakfast, John got a phone call. It was Bruce Walton.

"I got approval for you as Amy's foster parent," said Bruce. "I suggest you take her to the Copley Middle School and arrange for her to continue with her education. Tell them that she had schooling at the orphanage." That evening they went next door for dinner. John's wish came true. Sally made her special meatloaf. They enjoyed it very much. John gave Bill and Sally the details of his arrangement with the girls. At the school the next morning, the teacher questioned Amy's education at the orphanage. However, they accepted her in her old class but gave her the book and the assignments that she had missed. John and Grace planned on working with her to help her catch up with her classmates. The next week was Thanksgiving week. Sally and Bill invited John and the girls to have Thanksgiving dinner with them.

"You have invited us to your house many times," said John. "It is our time to invite you to our house."

"We would love to come to your house for dinner sometime. For now please come to my house. We have already purchased a large turkey."

"I feel like I owe you so much," said John. "At least I can give you a great Thanksgiving dinner. I'm a very good turkey chef."

"Please John, just this one time do it for me," she pleaded.

"How can I refuse when you ask like that?" conceded John. For the next few days John and Grace helped Amy study to catch up to her classmates. They soon became aware that she was a very intelligent young lady. Time flew by so fast that it soon was Thursday. They got up early in the morning and were eating breakfast when the phone rang. It was Sarah.

"Good morning Dad, and Happy Thanksgiving," she said. "How are you and my little sisters doing?"

"We are doing fine," said John. "I got Amy as a foster child and we are going next door with Bill and Sally for Thanksgiving dinner."

"Dad I'm so glad. I'm looking so forward to meeting them in person."

"You will soon if you come for Christmas," said John hoping for a positive answer.

"Dad, I can't promise anything yet. I have to catch up on so much work. I don't know if I can make it. I'm sure that I can get time in the spring."

"How are you going to spend your Thanksgiving holiday?"

"I've been dating this fellow surgeon. His name is Fred. He has invited me to have dinner with his family here in California. They live about an hour's drive from our office. Don't worry dad. There is nothing serious. We are just good friends that have our work in common."

"Honey, you deserve a family of your own, but I'd rather it be around here."

"Dad, have a nice day. Oh, before I forget. Do you remember Lee Young who I went to school with?"

"How could I forget," said John. "She almost moved in here with you. She used to call me Dad, remember?"

"Well, she is an Optometrist. She has opened an office in Cuyahoga Falls near route 8 off of Steels Corner road. I told her about Grace and she wants to see her tomorrow morning at eight. Grace's education in nursing and finance is what Lee could really use."

"That is so great honey, thank you."

"I have to go now. I have to get ready for the long drive. Talk with you tomorrow evening. Bye, Dad, love you."

"Love you too honey, have a nice day." John explained to Grace what Sarah had told him. Grace was so excited she could hardly stand still. At around eleven they went next door. The smell of the roasting turkey as they walk in made them especially hungry. They exchanged salutations, the girls hugged Sally and Bill, and they wished each other a happy Thanksgiving. When everything was ready they sat at the table and waited for Bill to say grace.

"You know," started Bill. "I think that we should do things different today. I think that each of us should give thanks to God. I will start and we will go around the table clock wise." When no one objected he started. He thanked God for all the success he had for the year. He thanked God for having John and the girls with them to share in the Thanksgiving meal. He thanked God for the food and he asked God to bless it. Sally repeated almost the same thing using different words. Next was Grace.

"Lord," she began. "I thank you for your love. I thank you for sending Mr. Cane to save Amy and me. I thank you for giving him such a big heart with love for us and wanting to be our earthly father. I thank you for such loving neighbors. I thank you for Amy who I love like a sister. I also thank my new sister in California who has found me a job." Next was Amy's turn.

"I Thank you Lord for such wonderful people like the Stevens. I thank you for the wonderful turkey that is so good. Most of all God, I thank you for my new daddy. In Jesus name I pray." John was so overwhelmed that the girls appreciated him so much that he felt tears wanting to come out of his eyes. He thanked God for all the blessing God had given him. For the wonderful wife he had given him for a short while. He thanked God for the wonderful and loving neighbors and most of all he thanked God for the wonderful blessing of having three most beautiful, sweet and loving daughters. John's tearful look was observed by Grace who because of it got tears in her own eyes. They ate the turkey with joy. They spent the rest of the afternoon with small talk. At evening, the girls and Sally had a small turkey sandwich. They watched a family movie that the Stevens had rented, which was more of a children's fantasy movie, but they all enjoyed it. Grace went to bed late designing a plan on how she would handle the financial business of a doctor's office.

The next morning John and Grace got up at six-thirty. John made breakfast, for Grace, who had to be at Dr. Young's office by eight. Amy didn't get up until nine. Amy and John ate together. About ten they got a phone call from their lawyer Bruce Walton. They were told that someone from the children welfare department was coming to talk with him about his adoption request.

"They will be at your house around ten," said Bruce. "Be prepared to be interrogated." Two ladies and a gentleman came around ten fifteen. They introduced themselves and requested a tour of the house. John took them through every room. John was happy that each girl had cleaned up her area and made the bed. John was sure to point that out. After the tour, they sat in the living room and John was bombarded with a ton of questions. John answered each question as accurately as he could. They seemed to concentrate on John's financial ability to support the girls. They asked Amy a few question that were obviously directed to getting a feeling on how happy she was to be there and how well she was taken care of. The last statement that Amy made was to say that she loved John as a true father. When they were finished they told John that they will probably be back for more information after they had investigated further and left.

"Boy that was a cold and stiff bunch," said John to Amy.

"They sure didn't seem friendly," added Amy.

Grace got to Dr. Young's office at about ten to eight. It looked like Lee had just gotten there herself. Grace waited for five minutes to get her courage up and went in.

"Come on in Grace," said Lee. "I saw you sit in your car for a few minutes. Trying to catch your breath I suspect. Relax. You were very well recommended. Let me show you around. That should help you relax and it will also show you some of the equipment you will operate to test the patients."

"Sounds like a good place to start," said Grace beginning to relax.

"I understand that your undergraduate study was mainly in finance, and then you went on to be a nurse but death in your family interrupted that pursuit."

"Yes, I wanted to have an undergraduate degree before I went to nursing school. My undergraduate major was biology. Finance was my minor subject, but I did well in it. I also have over a year experience as an assistant financial director."

"Tell me how you would handle my financial requirements?" Grace took out a sheet she had made last night, and explained how she would handle the finance of Lee's business. She explained how, using the system she had, would make it easy to calculate the costs and state and federal taxes. She explained how she would keep track of all daily costs and income and still have time for patient test that would be required. Once Grace relaxed, she rolled on to all details of her knowledge. "By the way," she said when she got through with her dissertation. "I already know how to operate most of the equipment you showed me. I read about some of them and took my mother through some." Lee took a big deep breath.

"You have the job," she said. "How soon cane you start?"

"When do you need me?" asked Grace her heart pounding through her chest.

"Yesterday," said Lee. "The other girls will come in about nine. We start at nine, take a half hour lunch, and work till five-thirty. I have a receptionist and an optician. I'm here at eight. You can start at eight if you want to get home earlier. When they got back to the outer office Lee reached in the desk and pulled out the current records. "Here you can start right now. Here are the statements for this year to date. I hope you can bring it all up to date."

"Shouldn't be a problem," said Grace. "I'll have everything ready for the end of the year statement." John and Amy waited for Grace to come home for lunch. When she didn't come or call by one in the afternoon they ate a sandwich each and decided to have a good dinner ready for Grace. John hesitated to call. He didn't want to disturb the interview. It was six thirty when Grace came home. She was all excited.

"Guess what?" she asked, but answered her own question. "I got the job. I started to work this morning," she said with great joy.

"Are you going to work till six-thirty every day?" asked John.

"No, that is the beauty of the deal. I can start at eight and get home about five. I'm late today because I stopped at the real estate office and asked them to evaluate my home with the plan to sell it." They ate dinner and there was great joy in the Cane house.

It was about two weeks later that John got a phone call. It was the real estate office. The agent told John that they had evaluated the property at around two hundred thirty-five thousand to two hundred forty-five thousand. She said that the chance of a sale around the holiday was small. She asked that they tell her how much they wanted to ask. On Sunday a week and a half before Christmas, after they set up the Christmas tree, the three got together and decided that they would want a clear two hundred thousand after all the fees, closing costs, and taxes. That would give them a better chance of selling the property.

The next week went by without anything new. Grace and Amy got a Christmas tree during the week and the three put it up and decorated it. Other than that, the days were all alike. Grace went to work, Amy went to school, and John being left alone went to spend some time at the soup kitchen. On Sunday December 21, John and the girls went to church in the morning. After getting home, they got ready for lunch. Before they sat down to eat, the phone rang. It was Sarah.

"Hi Dad," she said. "How is everyone? I'm sorry Dad; I just didn't get around to mailing you your Christmas gift. I shipped it today by special delivery."

"Honey, I don't need a gift from you. I thought we agreed a long time ago that we didn't need gifts. However, I do have a small gift here for you. I was hoping that you could get away for the Holiday."

"Sorry Dad. Tell me about the girls."

"They are down stairs in the recreation room. I got Amy one of those T.V. games and they are down there playing one of the games." John couldn't finish talking because there was a knock on the front door. "Could you hold a minute honey, there is someone at the door. Let me see who it is."

"Go ahead Dad. It's probably my gift. Go ahead, answer the door. I'll hold on." John went to the door and opened it. There in front of him stood a woman with a cell phone to her ear.

"Sarah" yelled John so loud that it was heard down the street. He set the cell phone on the entrance hall table and grabbed Sarah. His tears prevented him from talking.

"Can I come in?" said Sarah finally. Grace and Amy heard John yell so load that they ran upstairs to see what all the fuss was about.

"Girls," said John. "Look who is here. It's your sister Sarah." John introduced them to Sarah. They hugged each other like long lost sisters. It pleased John that they appreciated each other. They talked all night and the next day they shopped together and had a great time together.

It was on Tuesday two days before Christmas, when the subject of adoption came up.

"How is the adoption coming along?" asked Sarah.

"It takes a lot of time. We have been interviewed twice already and I'm sure it will not be the last," said John.

"I think he should only adopt Amy," added Grace. "I don't think it is right to adopt me."

"Why?" asked Sarah.

"Because I'm twenty three, I have not earned the right. I don't want to alienate you when a thousand years from now God takes Dad home."

"That is silly," said Sarah. "Why would your adoption alienate me?" asked Sarah

"It is because of the inheritance," said Grace.

"Look Grace," responded Sarah. "I'm a doctor. I have enough income and I already have a small nest egg. I'd rather have two sisters then a large inheritance. Besides, Dad is going to live forever. I'm not depending on an inheritance. It doesn't bother me. Anyway you could always decline your inheritance if it bothers you. However, I believe that you and Amy will need it more than I. Please don't decline sisterhood."

"Oh Sarah," said Grace with tears in her eyes. "What did I do to become part of this family?"

"You gave us your heart," responded John.

"I love you all so much," said Grace as she hugged Sarah.

"How about me?" complained Amy. "I love you too."

"We all love you too," said John. "And I think we would love to get something to eat. Sarah you are just in time." They all went into the kitchen to eat.

On Wednesday, the day before Christmas, the girls all went shopping. John had already bought gifts for the girls. He bought lockets for each girl. He had to print many pictures from his computer memory to get the pictures he wanted. He cut them to the size he wanted. Sarah's locket had pictures of Grace and Amy, one on each side of the locket when it was opened. Grace's locket had pictures of Sarah and Amy Amy's locket had pictures of Sarah and Grace. John had invited the neighbors, Bill and Sally, to have Christmas Eve dinner with them. They had a great roasted duck. They all enjoyed the food and had a warm time altogether. Especially happy was Sally who was instrumental in bringing such joy to John and his family. They spent the rest of the evening drinking coffee and eating four different kinds of Christmas cookies that Sally had brought.

Thursday, Christmas morning, John and the girls ate breakfast and afterwards sat under the Christmas tree and exchanged gifts. The girls loved their lockets. The girls got together and bought John a new computer with Skype.

"I love it" said John. "But Sarah has a computer with Skype. Why would I need another one there?"

"You don't understand Dad," said Grace. "This computer stays here. When you are here and Sarah is in LA, you will be able to see each other while talking with each other. When you are there, Amy and I will be able to see you while talking with you."

"I see," said John. "You don't want one for yourself?"

"Why would we need one?" said Grace. "Who would we contact except you and Sarah? We can use your computer when we talk to either of you."

"You can use a computer for many other things couldn't you?" said John to Grace. "Even Amy could use one for school work.

"Yes but I think you are going to buy me one for my birthday" said Grace.

"Oh you really think so?" said John with a smile. They all were happy with their gifts and enjoyed the rest of Christmas day together.

The next week Sarah went home. They couldn't talk her into staying for New Year. New Years Eve, John, Grace and Amy spent the evening together. After a great dinner they relaxed and watched the New Year's Ball in New York come down at midnight to introduce the New Year. On New Year's Day, John cooked a large ham. They celebrated it with their neighbors Bill and Sally.

The days after New Year became pretty standard. Grace went to work, and Amy went to school. They ate dinner together every Wednesday and usually lunch after church on Sunday. John spent Mondays and Thursdays at the soup kitchen. The winter was unusually mild. The days drifted slowly into months and it was soon Spring.

CHAPTER FOUR

The Disappearance

It was early March when Grace got John aside for a private talk.

"Dad," she started. "I have a little problem that I need to discuss with you."

"What is it honey?" said John with a frown on his face.

"Well, there are really two things I want to discuss. First I worry about Amy," she continued. "She will be out of school on June 8. I hate to leave her alone all day while I am at work. I would like to suggest that she moves in with you after school is out this summer. That means that if you plan on visiting Sarah, you should go soon so that you will be home before June 8."

"So you are trying to get rid of me," kidded John.

"You know better than that. I would rather you didn't go at all, but that wouldn't be fair to Sarah."

"I would love to have Amy move in with me. In fact, it would thrill me if you both moved in with me."

"I have another problem," continued Grace ignoring John's statement. "I met someone. He has taken me to lunch a couple of times. I think he is interested in me."

"How do you know he is interested in you? Has he said anything?"

"I can tell from the way he acts when he is near me. He kind of gets nervous and finds it hard to talk. I know he is very intelligent because he has been promoted to Sales Manager."

"How do you feel about him?"

"I like him very much. In fact I'm kind of ga-ga over him."

"What does he do?"

"He handles all the electronic devices used in eye examination. He first came to Lee's office to check on the new equipment and what we thought of it. Dad, he is a saved Christian, and goes to a Baptist Church in Chesterland."

"That sounds great but what do you want from me?"

"First, I trust in your advice, and I want you to meet him.

Secondly, I would like you to take care of Amy at any time I'm on a date with him."

"Of course," said John. "Let me know ahead of time so I can make time. You know that I have been going to the soup kitchen at different times as I'm needed."

"Thanks Dad. I know that he will ask me but I don't know when he will ask me. Paul has a sick mother in Cleveland. He goes there to take care of her after work every evening. He is negotiating with a caretaker who has Fridays free."

"Well it provides another reason; if I'm going to visit Sarah I have to go as soon as possible."

"While you are gone, I'll just invite him to dinner at my house. I would like to see how he and Amy take to each other, and I would like him to see what a good cook you have made me." It was on Friday the next week that John met Paul. They didn't have dinner at Graces house, but since John would be leaving for a while, John invited them at his house. John was very impressed with Paul, his outlook on life and his belief in God.

The next day John made plane reservation for Wednesday, since Wednesday was Grace's day off. The only time he could get reservations clear through to LA and back was a month later in mid April. He planned on a return on the Wednesday in early May. The day of departure came sooner that Grace wanted. Besides Amy and Sarah, he was the only one she had in the whole world. The flight was to leave at 9:20am. They asked him to be at the airport two hours before the flight. That would mean that he had to leave by 7:00am, allowing a half hour to get there. On Tuesday night before he was to leave, John invited the girls to a juicy steak dinner. It would be their last meal together for a while. John hugged Amy goodbye since she would be going to school. The next day, when Grace was to pick up John to take him to the airport, Amy declared that she was not going to school. She wanted to go to the airport to say goodbye to John. When Grace came to pick up John, he was surprised to see Amy in the car.

"What are you doing here?" he asked Amy.

"I'm sorry to disobey but I'm going to the airport with you." She said with conviction. They all got into Grace's car and she drove to the airport. After loving embraces all three found themselves with tears in their eyes. The girls felt a lonely feeling as they watched John go through security.

After John checked his luggage, got his boarding pass, he went through security and proceeded to the departure gate carrying only his attaché case. He had such mixed feelings. He was full of joy on the prospect of being with Sarah, but he was already missing Grace and Amy. He boarded the aircraft and found his seat. It was a window seat over the wings. He placed the attaché case under the seat in front of him and strapped himself in. After a few minutes a man came in a sat on the aisle seat. It seemed like all the people had entered when he saw a woman trying to set her carry-on case in the storage above the seats. He couldn't see her face but she had a nice shape. She tried the other side but couldn't find any room.

"Miss," said John. "Having trouble storing your case?" As she turned around and looked down to see who was talking to her, John saw her face. He instantly froze. He got butterflies in his stomach. He wondered if his heart had stopped. He had a lump in his throat. John heard himself talk but it seemed like someone else was controlling his voice. However he did noticed that she seemed flustered also. "Here let me help you," John heard himself say. "I think it will fit nicely under the seat in front." He heard her say something and handed him her case.

"Thank you so much," she said almost stuttering as she handed him her case. John easily slid it under the seat. The woman squeezed passed the man in the aisle seat and sat in the center seat. There were three seats on each side of the aisle. She looked at John and then looked away. Then as if to change her mind she looked at John.

"Hi," she said.

"Hi, how are you?" answered John realizing that it was a stupid remark.

"You are very kind to help me," she said after a while. "Thank you. My name is Loretta Winston, but my friends just call me Lora."

"Nice to meet you," said John getting back some of his control. "My name is John Cane. Are you going to Chicago on business?"

"No," she said with a smile that almost caused John's heart to skip a few beats. "I'm a nurse at a Cleveland hospital. I'm going to Los Angeles to spend a week with an old classmate. She has relatives in LA who got her a great job there. Are you going to Chicago on business?"

"No," said John thrilled at the sound of her voice. "I'm going to LA to spend time with my daughter. She is a Plastic Surgeon there, keeping the movie stars looking young. Actually her specialty is removing scars."

"Your wife not going with you?" she asked obviously wanting to know his marital status.

"No" replied John. "My wife passed away over a year ago."

"Oh, I'm so sorry," she answered. "You are too young to lose your partner so soon. You must miss her very much. But if you have a grown daughter you must be older then you look."

"I'm 48," said John. "And yes I think of her every day"

"I'm 43,"said Lora to John's surprise. Women generally don't give out their age thought John. "I know how you feel," she continued." I lost my husband 5 years ago."

"I'm sorry," said John, being really sorry for her pain, but also feeling a little relieved. "By the way, what flight are you on from

Chicago to LA? I enjoy speaking with you. It would be nice if we could fly to LA together." Lora looked through her documents.

"I'm on flight 1114," she finally answered.

"That's great," said John. "Let try to get seats together."

"We have one problem," added Lora sadly. "I'm on stand-by for the flight. I don't know if I will get on." John, now feeling more confident answered.

"I hope I'm not getting to bold, but I think that God had a reason to have us meet. I trust him."

"Are you a Christian?" asked Lora with a happy gleam in her eyes.

"Yes, I'm a born again Christian. I'm a deacon in a Baptist Church."

"Now I know that you are right," said Lora getting very excited. "I'm a born again Christian and I attend a Baptist Church in Broadview Heights.

"Is Pastor Barth still your pastor?" asked John.

"No, he decided to go back home to farm or something. I think, his father retired, or got too sick to work the farm. Do you know him?"

"Do you remember the large painting that hung as you enter the church?"

"Yes, it's a very large painting of Noah's ark with all the animals leaving the ark. I love that painting."

"Do you know the artist?" asked John.

"No, I don't remember looking to see who the painter was. Do you know who the painter was?" asked Lora.

"Yes," said John. "It was a man named Johnny Canelli." Then with an astonishing look on her face Lora asked.

"Was that you?"

"Yes, I have since changed my name to Cane. It was better for my writings."

"Are you Italian?" she asked.

"Yes both of my parents came from Sicily," answered John. "Do you have any Italians in your background?"

"I sure do," exclaimed Lora. "My mother is a full-fledged Italian. Her name was Maria Morelli. She taught me to be a great cook. You will have to taste some of my cooking. Then you will make up your own mind."

I'm surprised," said John. "I would not have guessed that you had Italian blood in you because you have such a light complexion."

"That's from my father's side. He was from Sweden. They are both gone now. My name of course is from my husband."

"I'll hold you to that dinner invitation," said John.

"Please do, was your wife Italian also?"

"Yes," said John. "In fact I think we were third or fourth cousins. My great grandmother and Annie's great grandmother had the same last name. It could be a coincident. However, they were all from the same end of the same town."

"I'm an incurable romantic," said Lora. "I would like to hear your love story. In fact I would like to hear your whole life story."

"If we get on the same plane in Chicago to LA, and get seats next to each other, I will do that on one condition. That is that you do the same."

"Why did you leave Broadview Heights Baptist church? You must have been there for awhile to provide a painting."

"After we moved to Fairlawn it was getting too far for us to drive." said John. "West Hill Baptist Church is only about five minutes from my house so we go there, well, I go there now"

"Please make sure your seatbelts are connected and prepare for landing," said the pilot.

"Look," said John, "If we don't get on the same plane, I would like to see you again."

"I would like that," said Lora. "Do you have a pen or pencil?"

"Yes," he said getting a pen from his attaché case and handing it to her. However, I have a card that you can have. It's my author introduction card. It has my name, address, and phone number on it."

"Aren't you a painter?" asked Lora in amazement as she wrote her name, address, and phone number on a piece of paper she found in her purse.

"No, that was only a hobby." The plane had just pulled up to the terminal. The plane had taken off and landed without John and Lora being aware that they had been in the air for an hour. When it stopped, people started to get up and retrieve their possessions from the over head racks. "I'll explain in my life story, hopefully when we get on the other plane." John and Lora got their cases from under the seat in front of them and held them on their laps waiting from the crowd to deplane. When the traffic was clear enough they left the plane. When they reached the terminal, Lora headed in the opposite direction headed to get a boarding pass. John headed directly to the departure gate.

"See you later," said John.

"I hope so." said Lora, "Call me if I don't make it."

John sat at one of the benches at the departing gate. He checked the itinerary above the departing gate to make sure he was at the right gate. Finding that he was at the right gate he relaxed. He had a one and a half hour layover. He kept looking down the hall way hoping to see Lora. John couldn't believe that he was so excited with a girl he had just known for an hour. He felt guilty. Annie had died less than a year ago. How could he feel this love for Lora? However, it seemed to him like he had known her all his life. He realized how much he missed her already. How could he wait several weeks to see her again if she missed the flight? He wanted to know so much more about her. He kept hoping and praying silently to himself, but the time went by without any sight of Lora. Finally his row number was called and he entered the plane and he found his seat. It was an aisle seat over the wings. He waited holding his breath but he didn't see her come aboard. Finally he heard the closing of the ships doors. His heart stopped beating. He felt sick to his stomach. He became very depressed. Why hadn't the Lord answered his prayer? He was about to give up when he saw her coming down the aisle carrying her small suitcase. His heart jumped from his chest. As she came by him he could see the joy in her face.

"I made it," she said with a happy smile. "I'm in the center seat on the left of the last row in the tail."

"That's O.K," said John. "Take your seat. After the ship is in the air and the 'Fasten Your Seat Belt' sign is off, I'll see what I can do." The plane took off and it seemed like forever, but the seat sign was finally turned off. John got up and walked to the rear of the plane. He found Lora seated between two middle aged men. Just behind her was a storage compartment. Across the aisle from the compartment was the rest room. There were three seats across the aisle from where Lora was seated.

"Hi," said Lora.

"Hi," said John. "I was so sure you didn't make it when I heard the ships doors close."

"I know," she said. "I just made it. They closed the doors behind me." John looked at the man in the aisle seat. He was reading some sort of document. The look on his face told John that he was upset at John's intrusion. John decided to ignore him. John looked at the man seated at the window seat.

"Sir," he said looking at him. When he didn't respond Lora tapped him on the shoulder. He looked at her and then to John. "Sir," John repeated. "Do you like to sit in the last row in the tail of the plane?"

"It's the worse seat in the plane," he responded with a disgusted look on his face. "I had no choice. I have to get to LA. Why do you ask?"

"I wondered if you wanted to change seats with me," said John.

"Where is your seat?" asked the man.

"I have an aisle seat in row D over the wing."

"Are you kidding me?" asked the man.

"No," answered John. "I would like to sit with my friend. Are you interested in changing seats?"

"Does a bear poop in the woods?" he responded.

"I guess that means yes?" asked John.

"You can bet your life on it," he said getting up and squeezing into the aisle. He retrieved his overnight bag from the overhead compartment and followed John to his seat. He checked the overhead compartment over John's seat, not finding room he then checked across the aisle. He finally found space and crammed in his bag. John grabbed his attaché case from under the seat and headed back to Lora.

"Thank you," said the man as John walked away. Neither had any idea the difference that move would make in the near future. John set his attaché case under the seat and sat down.

"I can't believe you did that," said Lora.

"I know you don't mean that," said John. "You knew that I would climb over each seat to get to you."

"Yes I knew," said Lora, "At least I hoped so."

"Isn't this the strangest thing?" said John. "We have known each other for less than two hours."

"I know," said Lora. "If I told this to my friends they would say I was crazy." John grabbed her hand.

"Do you still feel the magic?"

"More than ever," she responded. John noticed the love in her eyes as she spoke. "It seems to grow. I would have thought that it would diminish as we got to know each other."

"It's almost weird," said John.

"John," asked Lora, "do you believe in love at first sight?"

"Yes I do," said John, "I've only felt it twice in my life time, the butterflies in the stomach, the lump in your throat, but I also believe that it is very fragile. What a person is inside is very important. However, I believe that most of what a person is like inside shows up in their face and their actions, but we all have faults. We have to get to know the person before the love becomes permanent. We have to be able to accept the other person's faults. There are several things that a person may not be able to accept. You must make sure that the things that turn you off are not in his daily habits."

"What kind of things are you talking about?" asked Lora.

"Well such as, does the other person smoke does he drink too much and gets drunk often? You have to check off a list of things like this."

"Do you smoke or drink?" asked Lora.

"I don't smoke and I may have a half glass of wine with dinner," answered John.

"That's two checked on my list," said Lora. "What else do you think are important?" Everyone is different you have to evaluate with your own personality. One of the things a woman has to look for is what is his attitude? Is he selfish? Does he want to spend his life making her happy?

"I just checked off number sixteen," said Lora.

"Sixteen?" questioned John. "How did you get to sixteen? What is sixteen?"

"I've been checking you off all along," said Lora smiling. "I just checked off number sixteen. You were saying what the woman should be looking for, not what you are looking for. That shows that you are not selfish. You are thinking of the other person."

"What I'm just saying is that you have to get to know the other person."

"If that is true then I want to get to know all about you. So tell me your life story. We have several hours. I want to know every detail," asked Lora.

"You first," said John. "Then I will tell you mine."

"OK," she agreed. "But my story is short. There isn't much to tell."

"I'm sure you have a lot of wonderful tales to tell me," said John. "I'm an incurable romantic also. You will understand when I tell you about the books I have published."

"Wait a minute," said Lora with an astonished look on her face. "You're not Johnny Cane, the author of 'Love is everywhere' are you?"

"Guilty," said John.

"I love that book," exclaimed Lora. "I can't believe I'm seated next to the actual author. I thought your name sounded familiar but I never dreamed that it was you, wow, Johnny Cane. And you are interested in me? Give me a minute and let this sink in," she said looking at him in amazement. "I'm not worthy of you."

"Let me decide that," said John. "Now let's stop this foolishness and tell me your story. It may trigger a new romance novel about you and me."

"Oh," she said sounding nervous. "I was born on August 15th, 1970."

"You're kidding," said John interrupting her."That is incredible. I was born on August 15, 1965. We have birthdays on the same day. I'm sorry, please go on."

"That's fantastic," said Lora. "We can celebrate it together. Anyway, I don't remember much of my childhood. I remember that I met Florence in elementary school. Isn't it funny how we remember kids in elementary school, a few kids in high school, and hardly anyone in college? Flo and I became great friends. We kept in touch through high school and college. All I remember other than that is that we loved to play tennis. I met George in high school. He was the quarterback for our school football team. He was considered a great catch. We went together till graduation. I was made football queen on our last game. We were king and queen of our graduation dance. I guess I was impressed with the status rather than asking the question of whether we were compatible. I went on to the university. I took premed. I wanted to be an obstetrician. But when my father died I changed to nursing. I couldn't afford to go on to med school. I now realize that I love nursing. George took liberal arts, with a major in management. After we graduated we got married. That was in September 12, 1996. We were married 10 years when he died of a heart attack."

"You didn't have children during those ten years?" asked John.

"No, first of all we hardly ever saw each other. I became a widow long before he died. At first he got a job as a salesman for a major food chain. I was happy when he got promoted to sales manager. He didn't travel much at first. Then he got transferred to plant manager. I thought that was going to improve our relationship. However, he was assigned to reorganize plants that weren't doing so well. He was good at fixing plants problems. He would be gone for months at a time. Once I went with him to London. I rarely saw him and I was never so bored in my life. I don't particularly like to travel anyway. So I never went with him again."

"Is that really why you didn't have any children?" asked John.

"There were other reasons," continued Lora. "First he was a flash lover. Get on and off after his pleasure. I don't believe I told you that. He wasn't a very affectionate person. I need a lot of affection. Anyway, after he died I found out that he had his tubes tied so that he wouldn't have children. When he died I felt sorry for him, but I couldn't miss him. I'm not sure I really ever loved him. If there ever was any love between us it was more like brotherly love, especially at the end."

"That is terrible way to live," said John. "I understand how you feel."

"I'm really a very affectionate person," said Lora. "From what I already know about you, I believe you also are a very affectionate person." John moved his head in an affirmative action. "I really feel cheated," continued Lora. "I will never make the same mistake again. I need to love and be loved so badly. I have so much love inside of me that I think it's going to bust out."

"Great," said John, "let it bust out towards me. I loved Annie very much, don't get me wrong. But it was a different kind of love. You will understand when I tell you my story"

"Well, I think I'm done," said Lora. "I can't believe that I have told as much as I have. We have to get to know each other better, because I wonder if this 'love at first sight' I feel is true love or is it an overwhelming desire to love and be loved."

"I hope and believe it is true love," said John. "As for me I don't have that problem. I have loved and been loved. I already know all I need to know about you. I have never felt this way about anyone."

"That's because you have already heard my story," said Lora with a loving smile."

"Anyway, I guess it is my turn," said John. "As I mentioned before, I was born on August 15 1962. I only remember a few incidents of my child hood. I do remember an incident that occurred when I was nine months old. We lived upstairs from my aunt Stella. Across the stairway my parents had a folding wooded fence that prevented me from falling down the stairs in my 'Kiddy car' as it was called back then. I couldn't walk so it was my only mode of travel. One day my mother went down stairs for a cup of sugar. Since she would come back quickly and I was playing in the bedroom, she left or forgot to close the gate. When I heard her go down stairs I went to the stairs. When I saw the stairs and the gate open, I got an idea. The steps to me looked like a slide. It would be fun riding down the slide, so I took off. I was surprised that it was so terribly bumpy. The noise must have alerted the whole neighborhood. My father who was working outside came running in. As soon as he saw what happened he destroyed the 'Kiddy Car. I remember that because it was the worst part of the incident. Though I wasn't hurt I cried loudly because even though I was only nine months old, I was smart enough to know that the 'Kiddy Car' was my feet. It was like my father had broken my legs. My mother told me that right after that I started to walk. Am I boring you?"

"No not at all," said Lora. "I enjoy it very much. I can understand why you would remember that. It was a very traumatic time of your life. This is what I want to hear about you. It tells me so much about your life. Please go on."

"Well, there isn't much to tell until I was about 11 or12 years old. I got a crush on Theresa the girl next door. She was about my age. I remember getting a cowboy hat and a black mask. I played like I was Zorro. One day I got on the porch railing and yelled at Theresa who was just coming out of her house, 'Zorro comes to save you.' I remember that because I heard about it for months."

"That's what I want to know about you," said Lora. "I want to know every crush and romance you ever had."

"Well," continued John. "Theresa and I were given money to go to the movies on Saturday afternoon. The movie was located at the corner of our street. Once we went when a romantic movie was playing. We wondered why they did so much kissing. What was the pleasure in it? We decided to kiss every time the actors kissed to see what it was like. We kind of enjoyed it very much. One day we were sitting in my father's car and I kissed her. I then told her that I loved her and would she be my girlfriend. She said that we weren't boyfriend and girlfriend just good friends. I don't remember the exact words, but she indicated that she didn't love me that way. It broke my heart. Several months if not years later when we were older her cousin told me that Theresa loved me and asked why I didn't pay any attention to her. I told her that she broke my heart once and that I wouldn't let it happen again. I never forgave her"

"That's so sweet," said Lora. "I will have to remember that. I guess I would only get one chance. Please tell me more."

"I don't remember much of my younger days except that my friends and I rode our bikes a lot, played baseball in the empty lot behind the theater. I didn't date much in high school. I once dated a beautiful blond girl. She was the rage of the school. I felt so lucky that she accepted my request for a date. I took her to dinner and a movie. I found that she had no character or personality at all. But she had a very large ego. By the time I took her home she didn't even look pretty to me. I never dated her again. The only other date I had while going to high school was a girl I met at Kiwanis Lake. I was about 16 years old. I was there with three other male friends on a week vacation. Do you really want to hear this? I feel so foolish. It's like I'm bragging about my romances."

"Don't be silly," said Lora. "I want to hear every details of your life. I love it. Don't you know that I am living every moment of your life with you? It fulfills the feeling I have that I have known you all my life. Please go on."

"All right," said John. "But I want you to know that I feel a little uncomfortable doing this."

"Don't feel that way," said Lora. "Just think about how you are pleasing me."

"I had just gotten my driver's license," continued John. "My father let me borrow his car for the week. I met her on the lake. We kidded each other on our rowing abilities. I felt that we were both new at dating. I got her phone number and several weeks later I called her for a date. She gave me her address and we set a time and day. When I got there she introduced me to her parents who were just leaving. I asked her if she would like to go to the movies. She said 'No, Let's stay here and get acquainted. She told me that her parents wouldn't be home until late and that we would be alone. That scared me. Then when she sat next to me and started to kiss me passionately and rubbing her body on mine I panicked. It was only my second date I'd had in all my adult life. I wanted out so bad. But how could I do it without looking like a scared rabbit, which I was, or like an idiot. I remembered from experience with my sister, that women hate to be criticized. So I thought that if I criticized her she would cool off and try to be a normal date. I told her that her hair felt like straw. It worked better than I had hoped. She asked me to leave. I was never so happy to get out of a place as I was getting out of there.

"That is precious," said Lora laughing heartily. "I love your stories and incidentally, I love to hear you talk. Your voice thrills me." John understood what she meant. Her voice thrilled him also. "Please go on."

"The last date I had before I graduated was with a girl I met at a movie. There were three girls and three of us boys. We started kidding each other and I ended up with one of the girl's phone number. Her name was Carol. We dated for awhile, mostly double dating. I was afraid from my past experience to be alone with a girl. I did however take Carol to my graduation dance. One day we were at a dance hall in Vermilion On The Lake, which is east of Cleveland. My friend Jim and his date, who were with us, lived in the south side of Cleveland. So did I. It was 3:00 in the morning when we decided to go home. Carol lived near Vermilion. I started to drive to drop Carol off first being that she was close to where we were. She became very angry. She wanted me to drop the others first and then return to her house to say good night. It would have taken me over a half hour to drop Jim and his date off and another half hour to come back to Carol's house and then another half hour for me to get home. I would get home between 4:30 and 5:00 not counting the time we would spend saying good night. I had to be at school at 8:00 the next morning. So I took her home first. She was boiling angry. She slammed the car door and left in a huff. Saturday I went to pick her up to go to a party we had planned to go to. She wasn't home and her mother told me that she was worried because she hadn't come home the night before. To make the story short, I called the next week and was told that Carol had eloped with an old boyfriend. I was glad to get rid of her. She was too wild."

I think the lord helped you that time," said Lora. "She seemed to be very self-centered. I can't believe that her marriage will last too long."

"You are a very intelligent woman do you know that?" said John. "Six months later she called me and told me that it was a mistake and that she was divorced. She wanted us to get together again. I told her to forget it."

"Is that when you met Annie?" asked Lora impatiently.

"I'm getting to that," said John. "There were two other girls that I dated before Annie, one was very serious."

"Please go on," said Lora.

"After my first year of college, I went to work in Sandusky Ohio on a co-op program. There I met a very beautiful blond named Irene. We met on the tennis court. We dated for the four months that I was there. It looked very good for awhile. We even talked about marriage. However, when I returned to school I was too far away. She came To Cleveland several times, and I went to Sandusky several times. One day I got an actual Dear John letter. Lora, am I boring you? Do you really like to hear more? I could just jump to Annie."

"No, I'm sorry if I sounded impatient. I really want to hear about all your love life especially about the one that was very serious. Your life sounds fantastic; you have to write an autobiography. Please go on. I want to hear everything."

"Well alright if you really want to. Don't just say that to be nice."

"No I really want to hear it. I love the way you tell it."

"OK then," said John. "We do have a couple of hours to waste." Lora smiled lovingly. At the end of my second year at college, I met Cora. My friend Ray was going to college at Bucknell Universality in Pennsylvania. A friend in school gave Ray a letter to give to a girl the friend knew that was going to school in Cleveland. Ray asked me to go with him. She lived in the Christian Soldier's home for woman students. It was a very strict house. If a girl came in after 12:00 she had to be let in by the guard who then takes her name. Three times and they would call her parents. They would not let anyone upstairs to the girl's room. The woman at the entrance would call her and she would come down and meet you in the lounge. Cora was not in her room, but the woman at the entrance said that she was already in the lounge. When we walked into the lounge there was only one woman there. When I saw her I was petrified. I had butterflies in my stomach and a lump in my throat. My heart was beating out of my chest. It was love at first sight. 'Are you Ray?' she asked. Her voice rang out like heavenly music. I told her that I wasn't and pointed to Ray. I didn't say another word after that except I said goodbye when we left. I walked out of there floating above the ground. I had never felt that way before. The next day I called her and asked for a date. I was never so surprised in my life when she said yes. We dated for several months after which one day I told her that I loved her. She said that she loved me too. A couple of months later I asked if she would marry me and she said yes. I gave her a cheap ring with a fake diamond. I promised that when I got a job I would replace it with a real diamond. She said she didn't care that the symbol was all she needed. Besides she said it looked so real that no one would know. I took her to meet my parents. That didn't go as well as I had hoped. My mother wanted me to marry an Italian girl. Mon didn't speak English to well and was afraid they would not be close. Cora was Spanish. We were engaged for almost two years. We planned on our wedding for the next year letting me get settled in a job. After she graduated she went home in New Mexico. We sent chain letters to each other, that is that as soon as I got her letter I would write back and vise versa. I called her once a week. In late July she stopped writing. I tried to call her and she was never home to me. I finally got the picture. I was heartbroken. I cried myself to sleep, when I could sleep. I was offered a job at Clark Controller Corporation. I told them I would start in two weeks. I wanted to take my mother to Chicago to visit her cousins. I really wanted to get away for awhile to try to heal my heart. I felt unloved and unwanted. Aunt Nicolina, as I called her, had a dinner for us and invited her brother-in-law and his family to come and dine with us. They had a daughter named Anna Maria. It was obvious that she was interested in me. I was overwhelmed with her attention. That was what I needed. I needed to know that someone could love me. My mother invited Anna and her brother Salvatore to come to Ohio and spend a week with us. My mother and her parents noted that we were attracted to each other. Both families were pleased with the possibility that we would fall in love. I didn't feel for her like I felt for Cora. After two weeks in Ohio it was obvious that Annie was crazy about me. My choice at that time was of the mind not the heart."

"I don't understand," said Lora. "What do you mean of the mind?"

"What I'm trying to say is that I realized what a wonderful person Annie was, how affectionate and loving she was, but I didn't feel that I loved her. I still had Cora in my heart. But I also realized what a great catch Annie was. She had no other career or desire but to take care of her husband and children. Just before I decided to marry Annie, I got a letter from Cora. She told me she was sorry at how she treated me, and she wanted me to forgive her and take her back. She made one big mistake. She told me she knew how I felt because she had fallen in love with a friend of the family, but after several months he dumped her. If she had used any other excuse, I may have forgiven her. However her story told me that I was her second choice, her 'settled for' lover. I wasn't going to spend the rest of my life as her second choice."

"Good for you," said Lora.

"After that I proposed to Annie and we were married the next May. At first it was a bad marriage. I still thought of Cora. But Annie was a perfect wife and mother. Don't misunderstand, I love Annie very much. Although she started as my second choice I did have a choice, and I picked Annie. I realized how much I loved Annie when Sarah was born. I miss Annie very much."

"I understand," said Lora. "I wasn't as lucky as you. I never gave my husband my full heart. That was probably because he never gave me his. Anyway, is that the end of your life story?"

"There is more that you should know," said John. He then told her about his meeting with Grace and Amy, and his effort to adopt them."

"You said that you had the butterfly in your belly and lump in your throat twice in your life time. Once was Cora. Who was the second one?"

"That end of that story is still unresolved," said John. "I can't tell you about that. I don't know how that relationship will end. The outcome is still pending. The last chapter of that book has not been finished"

"What is her name?" asked Lora. Before John could answer a great lightening and loud thunder shook the Plane.

"Wow," said Lora getting excited. "What is happening?"

"While we have been talking we didn't notice that it was getting dark outside. It looks like we are flying into a heavy storm," said John vocalizing the obvious. Just then another lightening flashed at the same time that thunder seemed to hit the plane. The lights on the plane went off. The emergency lights came on as well as the 'Fasten Your Seat Belts' sign came on.

"Johnny," she yelled grabbing his hand.

"Don't worry," said John to Lora. "We are in the middle of a fierce storm. I'm sure the pilot has had a few of these in his career. I usually can tell how far a storm is from us by checking the time between the lightning and the thunder. Light travels much faster than sound. I think from this that the storm is on top of us." Suddenly, the plane tilted nose up which forced them against their seats.

"What's happening," repeated Lora with a voice full of fear.

"I think the pilot is trying to climb over the storm," guessed John. The plane climbed for several minutes then it turned clockwise away from its western direction and headed north. Lora's hand tightened John's hand. "I think now the pilot is trying to go around the storm," added John trying to keep Lora informed as to what was happening and anticipating her question. It seemed to be flying north for what seemed to be over an hour. It was obvious to John that the pilot was unable to fly around the storm. Suddenly lightning and thunder shook the plane violently. It was obvious that the plane was hit. The plane seamed to slow down from its forward motion.

"The wings are on fire," yelled Lora as she looked out the window. "Johnny she cried out. "Are we going to die?" John had been thinking about that. Would the Lord let them die so soon after getting them together? John started to pray to the heavenly father about what Jesus had promised. Ask the father in my name and believe that it will be given you and it shall. John asked that he and Lora would have more time together in the name of Jesus.

"I don't think we are going to die," said John in answer to Lora's question. "I don't believe that God would let us die after he took such an effort to get us together. The plane started to drop like a heavy stone. Suddenly the nose of the plane headed down so that the plane was now in a nose dive toward the ground.

"Johnny," yelled Lora wanting support from John.

"I think that the pilot is purposely diving to get aircraft speed," said John with a voice he tried to keep from trembling. "This way he can gain lift under the wings so to be able to land on a road or a field." As if the pilot had heard John he leveled the ship off a little. John looked out the window. All he could see were clouds and the heavy fire from the engines.

"Lora," he said "Put your head between your legs and your arms around your head for protection. The stewardess would have told us but I don't think they can because the power is off." Lora did as John asked. John looked out the window and saw that the plane had dropped below the clouds. All he could see were tree and mountains. Then as the plane flew lower just missing the top of the trees, John saw an open field. Hope rose in his heart. As the plane hit the ground the effect was much worse than John had expected. He was thrown forward, backwards, up, down, and from side to side so severely that his stomach hurt from the force against the seat belt. He tried to keep his head between his legs but the movement forces were too much. He couldn't control any part of his body. The plane's bouncing and swerving from side to side got worse. John began to worry about God's plan. His thoughts went to Sarah, Grace and Amy. How would they take the news of the accident? His last thoughts were of them. Suddenly the plane started to spin. As John tried to hold on his head hit the side of the plane just behind the window, and everything went black.

CHAPTER FIVE

Lost In The Woods

JOHN HAD NO IDEA HOW long he had been out. He felt great pain all over his body. His stomach hurt the most where the seat belt held him during the crash. He tried to move his arm but as he moved it he felt great pain in his right shoulder. He moved his leg. His knees hurt badly. He ran his left hand up and down his aching arm and leg feeling the bones as he was taught in the health class he had taken. They were very sore but he didn't feel any inconsistencies in the bones. Thankfully there didn't seem to be any broken bones. His attention quickly turned to Lora. The part of the ship they were in was on its side with Lora hanging over him held in place by her seat belt. He heard a painful sounding moaning. He reached up and felt her neck. To his relief she had a good heart beat. That told him that she was still alive. He did notice that the moaning didn't come from her. He pushed the seat in front of him with all of the strength he could muster. The seat fell forward and to John's surprise there was no part of the plane in front of the seat. There was nothing but open air. All he could see was a tree trunk which had apparently stopped that part of the ship, and about 100 feet in front of the tree he could see a large lake. Sticking out of the lake he could see a part of the ship which was mostly under water. John looked up past Lora. He saw nothing passed the aisle. The three seats and the Restroom on the other side of the plane were gone. He tried to get up but fell back down due to the movement of the part of the plane he was in. It was unstable. It looked to John that it wanted to upright itself, which was what John wanted. He stood up and tried to force the plane section over. He was unsuccessful. He grabbed the blanket they had given him and stepping on the arm rest he raised himself up so that he could throw the blanket over the sharp edge of the aisle structure. He worked his way over the structure and landed on his hands and head. He then reviewed the situation and found an extended piece of the tail that he could put his weight on to force the structure right side up. With great effort he finally succeeded. He placed a large stone on the extended piece of the tail to keep it stable. As he went around to the open end of the structure he heard the moaning. It came from the man at the aisle seat. John unhooked his seat belt and pulled him out onto the ground outside the unit. The man was fighting for air. He also had a large piece of metal sticking out of his chest. John didn't know how to help him. He didn't know whether to pull the metal out or leave it in. It didn't matter. He was too worried about Lora. He noticed that Lora's arm was broken between her shoulder and her elbow on her left side. He tied her broken arm to her waist with his handkerchief and the laces from his shoes to keep it from moving while he tried to remove her from her seat. He went to her right side. He grabbed her good arm and placed it around his neck. Carefully he lifted her and placed her on a blanket he had placed on the aisle way earlier. John checked her over carefully. It was obvious that her left arm was broken. He checked the rest of her body by running his hand down her arms and legs as he had done on himself. He felt a small crack on her left leg between the hip and the knee. He also found that she had blood on her left side. He also found a small cut on her forehead and a large lump on the back of her head. This worried him the most. He remembered reading about a sports figure that died days after he suffered a head injury. He opened his attaché case and found his packet of band-aids. He only had five band-aids. He looked around in desperation and noticed that the storage door of the compartment that was behind the seats they had been in was ajar. He tried to open it but it was stuck.

He looked around for a long piece of metal that he could use to pry it open. He was hoping that he would find something in there that would help him. He found a metal bracket and with a strong heave the door flew off and almost landed on Lora. He was quick enough to catch it and throw it outside the area. He looked inside the storage compartment and there sitting on a shelf that had been dislodged on one side was a large white box with a large red cross painted on it. It was a medical kit. Also in the compartment were several blankets and pillows. Beneath the shelf was a large role of heavy string.

"Thank you Lord," said John out loud. He opened the kit and found a bottle of Hydrogen Peroxide, a couple of rolls of gauze, some cotton, a large tube of Antibiotic Ointment, a small pair of scissors, and many packages of band-aids. He immediately went out searching for among the large area of wreckage, scattered all over to find a piece of metal that he could place as a cast on Lora's arm and leg. He almost gave up when he saw a small narrow strip of metal that had a small curvature along its full length. It looked like a small sliver of a large diameter pipe. It was a little over a foot long. That was too long by itself, but it had a bend about the middle of it. John worked the metal at the bend area back and forth and finally it broke in two. Using a stone he rubbed the edges of the metal to remove any sharpness. He then brought them to where Lora laid. He examined her again carefully. The break in the arm was the worst of her injuries. He placed his foot under her arm pit and pulled hard on her arm. He was relieved when he felt her arm snap in place. He quickly tightly wrapped the arm around the injured area with a few turns of gauze, not only to hold the arm together but to protect it from the metal he then place at the injured point. He wrapped several turns of gauze around the metal to keep it tightly in place. Next he did the same thing to the injured leg. He then lifted her blouse to examine the bloody area on her side. He saw that there was a deep cut on her side. He cleaned it with Hydrogen Peroxide and with a piece of cotton he coated the cut with antibiotic Ointment. He pulled the skin together, starting at one end, closing the cut and placed band aids crosswise along the cut to keep it closed. He then secured it with gauze around her body. Next he checked the blood on her head. She had a cut across the left side of her head. It was just beyond the hair line. He hated to cut her beautiful hair but he didn't have a choice. Using the small scissors he found in the medical kit, he trimmed around the wound as close as he could get. Then with his battery powered shaver he shaved around the area so that he could put band aids crosswise on the cut as he did on her side. He dressed it and closed it as he had done on her side and secured it with gauze at an angle from her right ear across the wound. He would have been pleased with his work if it wasn't for his concern for the large swollen bump on her head.

John turned his attention to the man he had pulled out. Upon examination he found that he had stopped breathing and had no heart beat. John checked around the area for other bodies. There was a woman and a man that was just in front of the section he and Lora were in. they were both dead. The other half of the tail was almost to the water. There were two passengers, a man and a woman, still strapped to the seats. They were both dead. Between the two sections he found a young man's body that looked like the male Flight Attendant. He also noticed two deep ruts that the plane had make as it slid into the lake. John felt that it would be a proper place to bury the dead. He checked around the area for something he could use as a shovel. Finally after about an hour searching he found a large flat piece of metal that was attached to a pipe. The metal was about eight inches by eight inched square. Using it, John dug in the ruts to make them as deep as he could. He searched the bodies for any possessions he could find. He could give them to the rescue team to at least identify those he had buried. He grabbed the two woman's purses and set them on the good ground away from the diggings. He obtained the men's wallets and rings and set them next to the purses. He was please to find that one of the men were smokers. He found matches and a lighter he decided to keep He was surprised to find a large six inch Swiss knife in the Flight Attendant's pocket. It had everything he could ever need. It had a screwdriver, a sharp main blade it had a can opener and a saw blade. Every so often he checked Lora. Her vital signs were good but she was still unconscious. He buried the women in one rut and the men in the other. He then shoveled a mound of dirt over them. He made two crosses from scrap metal and using the string to tie them together. He place one in each site. It was beginning to get dark so he returned to Lora and nestled next to her on her good side. He covered himself and Lora with a blanket. He went to sleep wondering and worrying about how badly his daughter Sarah, Grace and Amy were hurting.

The next morning John got up with the sun. He checked Lora. Nothing had changed. It was fairly warm for that time of year, so he decided to search the plane. He noticed that the plane was sinking deeper into the lake. If he had to retrieve anything from the plane now was the time. He grabbed one of the blankets and went down to the lake. He undressed and put his cloths and the blanket on a shrub nearby. He stepped into the water and he thought he would freeze into an ice carving. To reduce the pain and the length of the pain he took a deep breath and plunged head first toward the left side of the plane. That's where the entrance door was. When he got there the door was gone but the entrance was blocked by the service cart. He pulled it out and was about to throw it into the deeper part of the lake. He changed his mind when he saw the two wheels connected to a section of the cart. He decided that it could come in handy so he brought it on shore. He quickly jumped back in wondering how long he could tolerate the cold. Inside he searched the gallery. The drawers were all out in different positions. Some of the drawers were completely out and lying on the ground. One was full of soft drinks. Some were regular and some were diet. He brought that out and returned for other drawers. Some of the drawers were stuck and he had to force them out of the cabinet. He had to go in two more times to get the last drawer. One of the drawers had over two hundred nut packets and as many packages of plastic utensils. Each had a spoon, a fork, and a butter knife. One of the larger drawers had two large metal flat bottom bowls, two smaller plastic bowls and several plastic glasses. He struggled with that one but he felt it was very important especially to drink since Lora wouldn't be able to walk for awhile. Also he had no idea how long it would be before they were rescued. He came out of the water having no feeling in his body. He wrapped himself in the blanket and stayed that way for about fifteen minutes till he felt warm and dry. He put on his clothes and went back to Lora. He checked Lorna but nothing had changed. He spent the afternoon removing the end piece of the cart with the wheels and adding a flat piece of metal to the two protruding round pipes just above the wheels. This resulted in a small two wheel hand cart he could use to haul things around. He then returned to the water's edge and hauled everything back except the two soda drawers which he placed on a small under water sand bar to keep them cool. The rest he hauled up to their shelter where Lora was. He grabbed two of the large empty bags he had found in the larger drawer and placed the women's purses in one, and the men's wallets in the other. Any rings the women had he placed in their purses and the men's rings he placed inside their wallets. He was getting hungry so he had a can of soda and two bags of nuts. After it got dark he checked Lora then nestled at her good right side and fell asleep. During the night he was awakened by the sound of heavy lightning and thunder. He got up and checked the skies. It was dawn but heavy clouds were approaching from the north. John took two blankets and placed them over the edge of the structure. He found large rocks he could hardly lift and set them on the top of the structure to hold down the blankets. He also rolled heavy rocks on the bottom of the blankets to hold the bottom in place. That gave them protection on the left. They were protected on the right by the window side of the structure. He then grabbed a large piece of metal and placed it on the open side in front. He barely got inside when a heavy out pour of rain came down on their part of the plane. Lightning and thunder was so severe that it caused the structure to shake under the force of the storm. Although a little water got inside, John covered himself and Lora, cuddled up to her and tried to sleep. What else could he do? The storm had darkened the sky so that it seemed like midnight. The storm persisted all day. John had a soft drink and a couple of bags of nuts at about noon. It was about midnight the next day that the storm abated. By early morning the sun came out and the ground started to dry. John wondered how much the storm had delayed the search for them. He worried on how his girls were taking the news of the disappearance of the plane. He was hurting more for them than his own predicament. He trusted that God would take care of him. He prayed that God would give his girls the strength to survive until he was rescued. He realized that whatever happened he would have to find food soon or they would starve to death. John checked Lora. Her heart beat had almost doubled. John being worried hugged Lora and after a lengthy prayer began talking to her.

"Lorrie honey," he said calling her by a more affectionate name. "Please hang in there. I need you. Please don't leave me. We are safe now. I will take care of you." He repeated this several times and to his amazement her heart beat returned to normal. After he settled down for awhile and was certain that Lora was all right, he decided that he had to find food. "Lorrie honey, I have to leave you for a little while. I have to go out and find some food for us. Don't worry; I'll be back as soon as I can." He then took two plastic bags that he had found in the storage compartment. He assumed they were trash bags. He then traveled south away from the lake towards the mountain area looking for wild fruit trees, which he felt was unlikely. He was hoping that he would at least find some berries. He walked through the valley between the smaller mountains, through the woods and around the foot hills of the larger mountains. After walking a couple of hours he came to a very rocky area. What attracted him was a large rock which had slipped down the large hill and settled on the bottom. What interested him was its size and position. It was about ten feet wide and about twenty feet deep up the hill. It was fairly square and the front leaned forward at about a forty degree angle. He thought it would make a great lean to. He noticed that land above the rock was clear of trees and rocks and went up the side for over two hundred feet at an angle of about thirty-five to forty degrees. Above two hundred feet it turned into rocky ground all the way to the top. It would be a good place for a sign. He hoped that they would be rescued before that would be necessary. He also noticed that the trees at the foot of the large mountain south of him were of a different type. They were tall, straight, and had leaves different than anything he had ever seen before. However he felt he didn't have time to investigate that area at this time. He decided to return to Lora. He was about to pass the large open field when he spotted something yellow.

"It can't be," he said out loud. He walked over to the area he had seen the yellow flower and he was right. It was a field full of Mustard weed, commonly called Lucia by his family. John remembered how he had accompanied and helped his father go out into the country and pick Lucia. Just before they bloom into the yellow flower, they look like miniature Broccoli. There were many plants that hadn't blossomed yet so John was able to fill the two bags. He also noticed rabbit tracks. On the way back all he could think of was how he was going to trap a rabbit. When he got back, Lora looked like she had not moved. However the bandage on her head had come loose. John wondered how that happened. He checked Lora's heart beat and it was normal. He grabbed his two wheel cart and headed for the rocky area. He had already had a design of what he needed to cook the Lucia. When he got to the area he found four rocks about the size and shape he needed. He put them on the cart and on the way home he picked up as much fire wood he could find and put them on the cart. He got to the area he now called home about five o'clock in the evening. He set the rocks at four corners of a area that he wanted as his stove and set a large piece of flat metal 0n top of the rocks and set a fire under the metal. He then filled the large bowl with water and set it on the metal. He waited for the water to boil. When it started to boil he placed one half of one of the bags of Lucia into the water and waited for it to cook. He wasn't sure how long it would take so he tasted it ever so often to check it. While he sat waiting he heard a low moaning. John ran to Lora's side.

"Lorrie honey," he asked. "Are you awake?" she turned her head towards him.

"Hi Johnny," she managed to say with a low trembling voice. "How are you?"

"I'm fine," he answered kissing her on her forehead and the corner of her mouth. "How are you?"

"I have a severe headache, and actually I hurt all over. But I guess that is good."

"Why do you think it is good?" asked John confused at her answer.

"Because, I wondered if I was in heaven with a handsome angel looking down at me. However since I feel pain it must mean that I'm alive on earth."

"I'm not an angel and you sure are alive," answered John. "I was so worried that the bump on your head may have caused you to lose your memory or worse."

"So that's why my head hurts. I must have bumped it somewhere." John kissed her on her forehead, her eyes, her nose, and finally on the corner of her mouth. Somehow he loved the corner of her mouth. He felt the thrill down his back and into his stomach with the butterflies.

"How do you feel now?" he asked as he kissed her again.

All the pain went away as soon as your lips touched mine," she answered trying hard to smile. "You have to do it more often."After some thought she continued, "Johnny, why can't I move my arm?"

"Let me tell you of all your injuries," answered John. "First you have broken arm and a broken leg. I put a splint on both. They will be fine in a few weeks. You also have a deep cut on your side and a cut on your head. I dressed both with the medical supplies I found in the plane's storage compartment behind us. Then you have a large bump on your head that we already discussed. I took care of everything. You just need time to heal."

"What happened?" she asked. "Where are we?"

The plane crashed," answered John. "I have no idea where we are."

"Is the rescue team on its way?" she asked.

"I don't know what the story is on that," answered John shaking his head in a no motion. This is the fourth day since the crash and I haven't heard anything. I suspect that we are miles from the planned flight path. I remember the pilot turned north in his attempt to go around the storm. He couldn't tell the rescue team because the electricity was out and I suspect the radios were dead also."

"Have I been unconscious for four days?" asked Lora in amazement.

"I'm afraid so," said John. "I have worried out of my mind about you for four full days."

"You're a dear boy," she said with love on her face. "How many others have survived?"

"I'm afraid it's just you and me,"

"Dear Lord," exclaimed Lora. "God did answer our prayer and you were right that God brought us together for a reason. He wouldn't separate us now."

"Can I do anything for you?" asked John.

"I'm a little thirsty right now," she answered. John propped her up almost to a sitting position. He placed one of the drawers and two pillows behind her.

"How's that?" he asked.

"I'm a little dizzy," she said. "I guess that is normal after being on my back for four days. Give me a few more minutes to stabilize." John gave her some water from a soda can he drank earlier and filled with water to drink.

"How do you feel now?" he asked.

""I'm a little hungry now"

"I'm not surprised," said John. "I have some vegetable soup cooking. It will be ready in a few minutes."

"You're a wonder," she said. I think you could do anything."

"I couldn't bring you to consciousness," answered John.

"You know what?" she said being very serious. "You did help me. I don't know if it was a dream but I think I kind of awoke some time during those four days. I became frantic thinking that we were about to crash. Suddenly I heard your voice calming me." Lora then repeated everything exactly what John had said when he found that her heart had started to beat at a high rate.

"Oh sweet Lorrie," said John lovingly. "That wasn't a dream." He then explained what had happened. "I had no idea that you could hear me."

"So you see you helped me from going crazy," said Lora. I think that deserves a hug and a kiss"

"After you eat something, I will collect," promised John. While checking the Lucia, he asked her a question that had been in the back of his mind.

"Do you mind me calling you Lorrie instead of Loretta or Lora?"

"Loretta is the name on my birth certificate, but everyone calls me Lora. However my father was the only one that called me Lorrie. I loved when he called me that. I also love it when you call me Lorrie. It is so much more affectionate." John found that the Lucia was ready. He placed a small square piece of metal he had found before, on her lap. He grabbed a small bowl and filled it with Lucia with some of the remaining liquid that remained in the large bowl. He set it on the metal plate on her lap and gave her a spoon he had found in the drawer. She ate it and another helping. John ate the rest and then collected his reward till they both fell asleep.

The next morning, John got up early. It was the fifth day after the crash. His activity awoke Lora.

"Honey," he said to her, "I saw some rabbit tracks yesterday when I got the Lucia. I am going to see if I can catch a rabbit and at least get some more Lucia." John notices that Lora had a big smile on her face. "What's so funny," he asked.

"I just get such a thrill when you call me honey," she said. "Now go get us a rabbit." John took the string and set out to set rabbit traps. He set two at the end of the first field he had crossed. He set them at the end of the woods where he had seen the rabbit tracks. He carefully set the traps where the rabbit had to squeeze between a tree and a rock. He set two other traps at the field he had crossed near the rocky area. He then searched for stakes he would need to cook the rabbit. He decided that he would need two wye branches and a straight hard wood stick that he would put through the rabbit. The straight stick with the rabbit would rest on the wye pieces that would be pounded into the ground across the fire. He searched for a while and finally found exactly what he needed. As he walked past the rocky area he noticed that the wooded area on the right was so over grown with brier that nothing could get through. He wondered why only that particular area was that way. He walked up to the foot hills of the large mountain where the strange trees grew. They were so tall with thick heavy leaves that nothing could grow around them. John was about to leave when he noticed that one of the trees had died and fallen on the ground. There was no sign of leaves or green around it. John assumed it had been blown over by a strong wind and had been there for quite a while. He tried to break some of the branches for fire wood. It bent almost in half but wouldn't break. John suddenly realized that the Lord had led him there for a purpose. He checked for over an hour finding the two main braches he wanted. They were about three feet long with a slight bow to them. He then found about a dozen that were perfectly straight and about two feet long. He was amazed at how hard it was to cut the branches with the saw blade of the Swiss knife. He stripped off the bark and notched the ends. Using the string he made himself two bow and arrow weapons. He then walked back to check his traps. There was no success. He hid behind a tree and waited over an hour with an arrow in his bow waiting for a rabbit. Suddenly a rabbit appeared near the edge of the field about twenty feet from where John was hiding. John slowly pulled back on the arrow and let it go. He missed the rabbit which disappeared in a second. His arrow hit the ground a foot behind the rabbit and a foot short. It was obvious that he needed practice. Since it was getting late and Lora must be worried, he picked some Lucia and headed for home. It was apparent from the joyful look on Lora's face that she had been worried.

"I'm sorry I took so long. But since my traps didn't work I had to find the right wood to make a bow and arrow.

"I wasn't worried," she lied. "I knew you wouldn't leave me."

"I'll get the fire going and cook you some more Lucia. In the mean time why don't I go and get you a nice cold soda from the drawer I put in the water to keep it cold. The sugar in it will give you some strength."

"Sounds great," said Lora. John sat her up as he had done before and started the fire. He next set the bowl with water on top to boil. He then stashed the wye and straight pieces in a safe place for future uses.

"First I have to collect some more of my reward," he said as he sat down next to her.

"So you got addicted," she said with an accepting smile on her face.

"For eternity," answered John as he kissed her. The water was boiling long before John finished getting his reward. After cooking the Lucia, they ate and settled in for a long night. John knew when to stop kissing her. John had promised God, his mother, and himself that he would never dishonor a woman. He now promised Lora the same thing. He intended to keep his promise. He went to bed worrying and praying for his girls back home. He wondered how they would accept Lora.

The next morning John got up early. It was the sixth day since the crash and they had not heard anything concerning a rescue. To stay alive he had to get food. To do that, he had to practice using the bow and arrow. He hung a plastic bag from the low branch of the nearest tree. Using Lora's lipstick he drew target circles on the plastic bag. He practiced most of the morning. He learned how to compensate for the wind. At noon he cooked the remaining Lucia and promised Lora that he would have something better for dinner. He returned to the area he had seen the deer and rabbit the day before. He sat behind a rock for hours waiting for his rabbit. He was not going to give up. He had to get food if it took all week. He had no alternative. Lucia will not be available very long. He was ready to move to another place when he heard a sound coming from the other side of the rock. John slowly and as silent as he could be, pulled back the arrow on the bow ready to shoot. Suddenly behind the rock a deer appeared going for the water. It was a small doe. John released the arrow using the windage he had learned in practice. It flew through the air and pierced the deer in the neck. The deer fell over but soon got up and started to run. John's second arrow hit it in the stomach. John followed it through the woods and into the field. It finally fell over and died. John grabbed it by its rear legs and dragged it back to the river nearest to where he was staying. John skinned it, cut off its head, opened its belly and dressed it the best he could and laid it near the water. John planned on leaving most of the deer in the cold water but he needed some heavy string to keep it from floating down the river. He returned to where he had shot it. He untied the trap string and was ready to return to the deer when he noticed a rabbit coming out of the brush. It hesitated with its ears up listening for what had scared it. It hesitated too long. John put an arrow through its side. It fell over kicked a few times and died. John took down the second trap and with the rabbit returned to where the deer was. He tied the rear legs of the dear using double length of string. He pushed the deer into the cold water of the river and tied the other ends of stings to a small tree at the edge of the river. He threw the head, skin, and guts of the deer into the river which washed them down towards the lake. He knew that he should have buried the results of his dressing the deer but he didn't have time. He then dressed the rabbit the same way. He pulled the deer out of the water long enough to cut two slices of its flesh and brought them and the rabbit back to Lora.

"Wow," said Lora when she saw all the catch that he was carrying. "You hit the jack pot."

"When it rains it pours," said John. He started the fire and after the plate got hot he placed the two pieces of deer meat on it and it immediately started to sizzle. Using a piece of flat metal he slid it under the meat ever so often to keep it from sticking. He was hoping that the deer fat would also help. When it was well browned he turned it over. He helped Lora sit up as he had done before and got the two pieces of flat metal that he had chosen earlier to use as dishes. He placed one on Lora's lap. He cut Lora's meat into small pieces and placed it in Lora's dish. He handed her a plastic fork

"Thank you," said Lora adjusting herself so she would be comfortable.

"I think you can handle that," said John.

"You bet," said Lora. "It's a meal for a king." John then cooked some Lucia and they both ate with great pleasure. After they had finished eating John removed the metal plate from the fire using some sticks he later put in the fire. He pounded the two wye branches, one on each side of the fire, into the ground. He stuck the longer branch through the rabbit from rear through its body and out of its neck. He set the branch with the rabbit on the wye units. He continued turning the rabbit over the fire to make sure it cooked evenly.

"Doesn't that look and smell good?" asked John.

"Yes," said Lora. "But why are you cooking the rabbit now. I couldn't eat another bite."

"It looks like a storm is coming," answered John. "I think we should have rabbit tomorrow, hot if we could heat it or cold if it rains. Also I noticed that this section of the plane is getting closer to the lake. I think the lake is growing. Its spring and up on the mountains the snow is melting. The lake is now up over the crosses I placed on the head of the graves. I think I will have to find us a new home. If the weather permits I will leave early tomorrow to build us one on higher ground towards the mountains" After the rabbit was cooked John cut it in pieces and set it in the large bowl. "If I don't get home till very late or possibly the next day, you will have plenty of food," said John. "I will also place a few cans of water and soft drinks at your side. You should be fine."

That night the storm that John had predicted from the look of the sky the evening before, raged with great fury. John went to sleep thinking of his three daughters. He wondered how they were taking his disappearance. The next morning the sky cleared. It was the seventh day since the crash. John got up early and got ready to travel. As he was about to leave, it suddenly dawned on him that he had to set thing up so that Lora could sit up or lay down by herself. He attached a metal bar from the seat under structure to the structure over Lora's head so that with her good arm she could pull herself up.

"Honey," said John," I'm sorry that I have to leave you. I'm leaving you a bow and arrow for your protection. You will have the rabbit, water, and soda. I will leave them here next to your good side. Will you need anything else?"

"No, I'll be fine,' said Lora. "Perhaps you could leave me an extra small bowl for medicinal purposes.

"Of course," said John. "Do you need anything else?"

"What are you going to eat?" said Lora ignoring his last statement. "Why don't you bring some of the rabbit with you?"

"No," said John. "I'll find something along the way. I also have a couple of nut bags with me. I have too much stuff to carry"

"Go then," said Lora "Go build us a home." John kissed her goodbye and headed south to where he had seen the large rock. On the way he dragged a large piece of the wing he had seen the first time he came to the rock. He planned on it being the roof of their new home. He dragged it up to the large rock and with great effort and much time; he finally succeeded to place the flat side on the rock. The other end which had a slight curve along its length sat on the ground. John next measured the height of the rock from the ground using a length of string. He then added about a foot to the length. He searched through the woods for four small trees that he could cut to the size of his string measurement that he could use as posts for his building. After finding them and cutting them using the small saw on his Swiss knife, he cut a v notch on one end of each pole. He then lifted the wing off the ground and with great effort slid it further onto the rock. He then holding the wing on his head slipped one of the poles under the center of the wing so that the curvature of the wing fit into the notch of the pole. He then pushed the pole to an erect position lifting the wing to a height slightly higher than the stone. He tied a small rock to a piece of string and held it from the edge of the wing. This gave him the location he wanted for the poles. He dug four holes about a foot deep where he wanted the poles located. He placed the center pole in the hole and removing the first pole which held the wing higher than needed. The wing dropped into the notch in the pole and settled at the height of the rock. He then placed the end poles in the holes and in place on the wing. Lastly he placed the other poles in the center of the wing about a door way distance from each other. Next he climbed up the mountain and looked for two large rocks. Finding them, he rolled them onto the wing to hold it down on the base rock. He had to use the metal unit he used as a shovel to pry the rocks down to the wing. He spent hours searching in the southern crash area where the plane left most of the wings and tail. He was looking for flat pieces of metal he could use as sides against the posts. Flat pieces had become scarce. He places a piece against the two posts on each end of the side opposite the rock. That left a door way facing the west side. He placed a piece on the south end of the structure. He left the other end open for the lack of metal. He would have to find something later. For now he would cover it with a blanket, holding it down on top and bottom with heavy rocks. When he had finished he headed back to Lora. It was starting to get dark. It was a little over an hour walk to get to Lora. On the way he found the last of the Lucia. Most of the plants had flowered, but John ate it anyway flower and all. He was able to pick enough to take back to Lora. When he got there it was completely dark.

"Hi," said John. "Why are you sitting up? Are you having some problems? Are you having problems sitting up and lying down?"

"No," she answered. "I just got up. I was tired of sleeping and being on my back. I can't turn to my side to easily or very much. I would really like to try walking around a little."

"It's late now," said John. "Besides I am very tired. I have worked hard to build us an acceptable living area. I will make you some kind of crutches tomorrow and get you walking some.

"Great," said Lora. "I left you a rabbit leg. It is there in the bowl."

"I sure could eat some. I eat some Lucia on the way here.

"How did you cook it?" asked Lora.

"I didn't cook it," said John. I ate it raw. It was a little bitter raw but it was still enough to get me here." He ate the rabbit leg and, after some small talk, arm in arm they fell asleep.

John went out early the next day looking for wood to make a set of crutches for Lora. It was the eight day since the crash. The sky was clear and the temperature was comfortable. He finally found two wye branches long enough to do the job. He cut the wye branches a little longer than needed. He then set one under Lora's arm and set her hand down to mark where the hand would reach on the wye to determine the place the cross handle should go and also where to cut the wye branches to the correct length. He then marked the straight section at the end of her feet. Lora was still asleep when he did this. Suddenly Lora woke up wondering what was happening to her.

"I'm sorry to wake you," said John. "I'm just measuring you to make your crutches. He cut the branches to the length as marked. He cut two holes on each crutch piece at the points marked for the hands. He cut two straight pieces so the diameter would fit tightly in the holes. He then pounded them through both holes to make a place for the hand to grab. He did the same thing at the top of the wye so that it would support the body weight by way of the arm pits. He did this for both crutches. He helped Lora get up and taught her how to use the crutches. They walked around the area until Lora felt comfortable with them. John was as delighted as she was at her progress.

"You did such a great Job at making these crutches," said Lora. "I think you can do anything."

"Thank you," said John. "I wish that was true. If it were we would be home by now. Anyway, listen honey, it is almost noon. This section of the plane, as I'm sure you have noticed, has freed itself from the tree and is slowly sliding down toward the lake. We have to move right away."

"I know," said Lora. "Set me down and go do what you have to do. I'll be all right."

"First I will start a fire, and before I leave we should eat. I don't know if we will have supper this evening." John started the fire and went to the river and got two large slices of deer meat. After they ate John helped Lora lay down in her bed He took the two wheel cart and loaded it with whatever he could carry. He took the purse bag, the wallet bag, the nut drawer with the nuts and silver ware, the soda drawer, and the medical kit. He also took all but one blanket and one pillow. He left Lora two cans of soda, and two cans of water.

"Go already," said Lora. "I'll be fine. I have all I need."

"It is now twelve-thirty," said John. "It will take me a little over an hour to get there and a little over an hour to get back. Adding a little time there I should get back around four to get you. Be ready to travel." John then left with his load. He got there about an hour and a half later. He placed everything safely at the far end of the structure. He dug a hole where the rock touched the ground and stored everything there except the drawer with the soda. He placed it in the river across the field nearest to him. He returned around four as he had promised. He found Lora coming out of the woods.

"What are you doing walking around especially in the woods?" asked John being concerned for her safety.

"I had private business to take care of," she said blushing a little. John decided not to pursue it any longer. He got a large piece of metal he had previously placed on the side of the tail section to keep out the water and placed it on the two wheel cart. After placing a blanket and a pillow on it he helped Lora climb on to it. The remainder of the bowls, the glasses and other necessities he put on her lap. Slowly he pulled her up the hills and across the fields. Since some of the trip was up hill it took longer than John would have liked. They arrived at their new home at about five. He got Lora settled in and had her sit up. She had no trouble. John tied four nylon stings to holes in the wing structure so they looked like two small swings. Then he asked Lora to extend her arms as high as she could. He then adjusted the length so that Lora could read them.

"Now Lorrie honey," he asked. "See if you can reach them and pull yourself up to a standing position." Lora grabbed the strings with her good arm but didn't have the strength with her bad arm. Use your bad arm just for balance, so that you don't fall over just using one arm." She struggled a few times and finally found that she could pull herself to a standing position with little trouble.

"Johnny," she said with joy in her voice. "You're a genius."

"Your crutches are leaning here on the rock where you can get to them easily. I have to go back to get our stove," said John with a chuckle. "And I will have to go back later or tomorrow to get our deer if we want to eat. I'll go now. Don't wander to far from here."

I won't," she promised. "Hurry back." It was after eight when John returned and it was getting pretty dark. John had picked up two slices of deer meat while there. John set up the stones and the wye branches as they had been down by the lake. He quickly started a fire and cooked the meat. They would be eating late but John wasn't sure when they would eat again. After they ate they snuggled together in the beds enjoying their new home. Although John loved to be in Lora's embrace his thought always went back to Sarah and his unofficially adopted daughters, Grace and Amy. He not only worried about them, but now he started to miss them terribly.

CHAPTER SIX

Surviving In The Wilderness

THAT NIGHT IT STORMED ALL night. It was the worst storm they had yet. The lightning and thunder was so severe that John thought they were being bombed. It was the wind that he was most afraid of. It rattled the wing so that John worried it would fly away. Neither John nor Lora slept that night. Fortunately it didn't last all night and in each other's arms they fell asleep.

The next morning it was still raining. The lightning and thunder was very slight and sounded like it was far away. It didn't stop raining until ten-thirty. John got up and after kissing Lora he set out to get the deer so they could have something to eat. He took the two wheel cart to carry the deer in. When he got there he loaded the deer and pulled out the metal stake so that he could use it at the river's edge near where they now lived. When he started back he decided to take a last look at the tail section where they had stayed the first eight days after the crash. He wanted to make sure they got everything. It was gone. It had washed down to the lake during the violet storm. He got back about two in the afternoon.

"We moved just in time," he told Lora. He explained what he had seen.

"I'm getting hungry," she said. "And I am getting tired of deer."

"Boy! now we are getting particular are we?" John said in jest. "Eat deer just one more time and I'll get you something different."

"Can you still get Lucia?" asked Lora after they ate the deer meat.

"I'll check as soon as I get the rest of this deer in the river. However I'm sure the Lucia season is over. I'll try to find some soft flowering stems that I think are eatable." After putting the deer in the river, tied it to the stake, he went to the area that he had obtained Lucia before. It was the same place he had seen the rabbits. As luck would have it, he saw a nice fat rabbit. He shot it through the belly. He checked the field where he had gotten the Lucia before. He was sure that the season for Lucia was over, but he remembered something his father had told him. He had said that if you pick the bud of a lot of Lucia it will grow another sprout again even after the season is over. As it happened John was able to fill a bag of new growth. That evening they had both rabbit and Lucia for dinner. They had enough of both left over to feed them at noon the next day. After eating lunch Lora had a question.

"Johnny," she asked. "This is the tenth day we have been here. Do you think they have stopped searching for us?"

"Gosh," he answered. "I don't know. We are probably so far off the flight path, that even if they were still looking they could never find us. I think we are like the needle-in-the-hay-stack. "Give me time. I think I have an idea on what we need to do. Trust me. What is your hurry anyway? I'm taking good care of you here."

"I trust you completely, she answered. "It's just that our relationship is at a standstill here."

"You mean that there is no preacher here," said John with a great big smile on his face.

"You said it not I," responded Lora. After that John grabbed his bow and went hunting. With God's help he was able to get a rabbit and a small deer that afternoon. He dressed them and put them in the river to stay cold.

"We now have enough food for a few week or more" said John when he got back.

"Isn't there any other type of animal we could catch to eat?" asked Lora.

"So now you are even tired of deer and rabbit, and what do you mean "We could catch'," said John kidding her.

"Just asking," she responded.

"I could climb up to the top of the mountain and see if any mountain goats live there," said John. "But for now I have another more important task I have to do. This is the tenth day that we have been here. If they are still looking for us they can't continue much longer. I have to see if I can set up some kind of a signal or sign to help any rescue planes that are looking for us find us." John then climbed up to the field above their living quarters to measure the flat area. He paced it off his stride being approximately three feet. He found that it was seven strides across or twenty-one feet wide and five strides up the hill or fifteen feet deep. He then sat down and figured what he needed for the largest sign he could place in that area. He determined that he would need five straight logs about six feet long and about six inches round. He also determined that he would need eight pieces about two feet long of the same diameter and he would also need about forty-five stakes to hold the logs in place.

The next morning he went out into the forest to first find the long logs. It was difficult to find the right thickness and of the right length and straightness. The first day he only found three trees that met the requirements. With the small Swiss knife saw blade it was difficult and time consuming to cut down the trees and then cut the pieces to the right length. It took him seven days to get all the wood at its required size. John got into the habit of scratching a mark on the rock inside their dwelling area. He wanted a running number of how many days they have been in the forest. Lora was starting to move around regularly.

"When are you going to remove these things on my arm and leg," asked Lora. "The areas are starting to itch."

"It has to be at least three weeks I believe, and it has only been eighteen days" said John looking at the markings on the rock wall.

"However it is time to remove the bandages from your side and forehead. I changed the bandages twice when you were unconscious. Now I think we can remove them permanently. Please lift up your blouse so that I can remove that one first. It was the worse of the cuts." Lora did as John asked. John carefully removed the gauze that was around her body first. Then he removed the tapes. It would be the more painful part of the procedure. Then he removed the rest of the bandage. The cut was completely healed. Only a tiny scar was noticeable. Next he removed the bandages from the forehead. It was almost loose anyway. The hair had started to grow back lifting the Band-Aids. There was no scar visible. "There," said John. "You are as good as new. Right now I have to go finish the sign." John brought the five long straight logs up first one at a time. They were very heavy and he struggled to get them up there. He set the first two about two feet apart. He set the next one two feet from the first two. He then set the other two four feet apart from each other and four feet from the other three. They were all set up hill across the field. Using a stone that he found that he could use as a hammer, he staked them all at the bottom to keep them from sliding down the hill. He then placed two stakes on each side two at the top end and two at the bottom to keep them from moving out of line. He then brought up the eight two feet logs. He set one in the center between the first two logs to form an H. He staked them in with four stakes, two on the right and two on the left. Using the same procedure, slowly day by day he formed the E and the L. On the sixth day he set the last three two feet logs at the top of the last long log to form a P.

It was now around the first week of May. Lora was walking pretty well using a cane John had made for her. John looked at his markings on the wall he called his calendar. It was now twenty-one days since he had taped the metal pieces on Lora's arm and leg. That morning when they woke John informed Lora of his decision to remove the metal piece from the leg. That would help by removing some of the weight. She was thrilled and excited. He removed only the metal from the leg, since it was not hurt as bad as the arm. He wanted to keep the arm bandaged a little longer because the bone had actually separated. He wrapped the leg tightly with gauze just to make sure it was really healed. The next day John stayed in bed until late morning. He could think of nothing but the three girls that he loved so much. He wondered what they were doing and how hard they were taking losing him. By now they must believe that he was dead. He forced himself out of bed. He had planned to climb the mountain to see if there were any goats, but it had rained most of the morning. After the rain stopped John decided to get some deer meat for lunch. Lora was starting to insist that she do some of the cooking and it would be noon in an hour. When he got there he was surprised at what he saw. A fairly large fish was trying to nibble on the deer meat. He quickly tied a string to an arrow and shot the fish through the body. He pulled it to shore and though it wiggled about a little, it was obviously dead. He scraped off the scales and dressed it ready for cooking. He returned to their living quarters and he found that Lora had already started a fire.

"You must be pretty hungry," said John kidding her.

"I'm just so excited that you are bringing me a delicious lunch for a queen. What is it? Is it a Tender venison steak? Or perhaps it's a fat tasty rabbit leg. I can hardly wait," kidded Lora.

"I guess you are tired of deer and rabbit meat," said John.

"Do you really think so?" said Lora being facetious.

"I agree with you," agreed John. "What kind of a friend have I been? I'm so sorry. I'll make it up to you. How would some fresh tasty wild fish suit you?"

"John," she said looking hurt. "That wasn't very kind."

"Are you saying that you don't want any of this?" said John showing her the fish he had in his bag. Lora was so shocked that for awhile she couldn't talk. She then threw her good arm around John tearfully.

"I should have known better," she said. "You have never let me down." After they cooked the fish they ate it with great satisfaction. That evening they slept with contentment.

The next day before John went climbing up the mountain to see if he could find some goats, he fastened one of Lora's hair pins into a fish hook. He placed a piece of dear meat on the end and tied it to a piece of sting. He then threw it into the river and tied the sting to the stake near the deer's body. He then left to climb the high mountain nearest to them. He returned about two in the afternoon. Lora had a fire going with the last of the rabbit cooking.

"I thought you would be home soon," said Lora. "So I started to cook us some lunch. Did you see any goats?"

"No, I didn't see any sign of any animal up there. I think I will have to go south to the denser mountain area. I think there is a mountain in that group that is a lot higher than the ones around here. I'll go there tomorrow. I will have to leave at the break of dawn. Later that afternoon, John went to get some deer meat and check his fish line. He was extremely pleased and surprised to see that he had caught a nice size fish. He didn't believe that his crudely fastened fish hook would work. He dressed the fish and took it to Lora.

"Wow," said Lora. "You got another fish I see. That's two great dinners in a row.

"You are worth it to me," said John.

"That's so sweet," said Lora. "When do you think you will be home, tomorrow? I can try to have some food for you."

"You know I have second thoughts on that," said John. "I checked the deer when I got the fish. It was only a small doe. We have a little meat left. We are out of Rabbit, and all we have is this fish which we will eat tonight. I don't think this is a good time to go hunting something we are not even sure exists. I think I will put it off for awhile. I'll go hunting tomorrow and stock up on some food. Where I will be going is pretty far. It will take me about two hours to get there, and about two hour or more to climb and search for goats. Even if I catch one it will take me two hours to get home. I would have to leave about six in the morning and wouldn't get home until late in the afternoon at the earliest. I can't leave you alone without food."

"Whatever you say," responded Lora. "I wonder if it would be worth it anyway. We could do without goat meat."

"I wasn't thinking only of goat meat," said John. "I was thinking if I could catch a nursing female goat we could have some goat's milk for breakfast."

"Oh Johnny," said Lora. "What chance do you have of doing that?"

"Just a thought," said John. "It's that I want some milk so badly. And that is another reason for my delay in going. I have to design and build some kind of a trap for the goat. It would only work if they travel in herds so I can pick the goat I want to trap. However since I'm not sure where we are I don't even know if there are any goats in this area. They are usually in mountainous areas.

"I think you are right," said Lora. "You have to check it out."

"Right now let's relax," said John. "Tomorrow I will go hunting for rabbits and a deer." They spent the rest of the evening with passionate kisses and romantic conversations. The next morning John went to the field he had caught deer before. He hid behind a tree and waited for nearly two hours. Not a sigh of a deer. He moved to another location and waited. No sign of a deer. It was almost noon when he spotted a small rabbit. He shot it and took it back home. It was better than nothing he thought. He decided to go back to Lora

"I think we have scared all the dear in this neighborhood," said John. "Perhaps I should go later about dusk. I remember back home that we had to watch out for deer in the evening"

"That little rabbit will be enough for today," said Lora trying to comfort him. "Maybe you will get a deer tonight. Let's eat the rabbit." They cooked the rabbit, fed themselves and later that day John left to hunt a deer. He came back around ten without a deer.

"I think tomorrow I will have to go back to the lower field near the lake."

"Maybe you should go up to find a goat," suggested Lora.

"No," said John. "I don't want to leave with so low of food supply. I want to find food down here first. I will go back to the lake and at least I think I can get a couple of rabbits. I also want to try and catch more fish although without the deer meat down there, I don't know right now what I will use for bait."

"I'm not concerned," said Lora in encouragement. "I trust that you will figure something out. Maybe you will find some worms for your fish hook."

"Well the Lord got us here," said John. "He is the one we both should have faith in."

"Amen" said Lora. They repeated last night's behavior.

The next morning John got up at dawn. He decided to go to the place he had found dear before. He was going to get a deer or large rabbit if he had to stay there all day.

"Listen," he told Lora. "There is no reason for me to come home at noon without a deer or rabbit. We don't have much to eat here. I will leave you some nuts and some soda. I will bring about three cans up here before I leave. The sodas have lots of sugar. That will keep you with some energy. He kissed her and after getting the sodas he left for the field he had hunted before. It was about one when he did have a chance to get a fairly large rabbit. Happy with that he went home.

"Hi," said Lora happy to see him. "I see you got a rabbit."

"This rabbit will only feed us now and tonight," said John. "We need a deer to feed us for many days and also supply us with some meat for our fish hook."

"One day at a time," Lora answered. "The Lord will help take care of us."

"I'm going to try one last time tomorrow," said John. "I am going all the way down to the lake. The deer are feeding and drinking somewhere on the river or perhaps on the lake." They ate the rabbit at noon and finished what was left that evening. That night it rain heavily all night. The next day he went down to the lake. The land was very wet and some areas were muddy. That made John very unhappy until he got there. Right at the edge of the lake he saw about a dozen worms. He took as much as he could get and placed them in a bag he always carried with him. He then hid behind a bush and waited for a deer to come to drink water. Twice he saw deer but he was not hidden enough to be able to shoot one. As soon as he brought his bow up they disappeared. That afternoon he went back to the area he kept the deer. He figured that the fish would go there looking for the food they had found before. He didn't know if his theory was correct but he did catch a large fish. It was still early afternoon so he tied it to the pole he had used before and cast for another fish. He caught two other fish before he returned to Lora with one of them.

"How would you like a fish for dinner?" he asked.

"Sounds great and as you can guess, I'm very hungry." She answered.

"I also left two more large fish in the river across from us. You can get one each day if I don't show up tomorrow. I am going to head south down the river to get a deer or a goat, even if I have to climb up one of the mountains. After they cooked and ate the fish they went to bed early. The next day John got up early and headed south towards the larger mountains. He passed the woods that were impregnable due to the barberry, and circled around the mountain that was south of the woods. As he came to a field just before he reached the mountain he wanted to climb he saw deer tracks all over the field. Just passed the field was a small clump of trees that led to the river. He slowly went to the trees and hid behind one that had a shrub growing next to it. He waited for about an hour when a couple of deer showed up crossing the field toward the water. Slowly and as quietly as he could he raised his bow. The deer noticed the movement and hesitated. It hesitated a little too long. John got it in the neck. The problem he had now is to get it to the lake across from their living quarters. With much struggle and a few stops to rest he got the deer to the lake and tied it as he had done before. After skinning it and dressing it he cut two slices of meat and headed across to their home. When he got there he heard Lora screaming his name.

"Johnny," she was screaming, "Help me." She yelled several times. She was at the very other end of their structure up against the rock. John ran to her yelling back at her.

"Lora," he yelled. "What is wrong? I'm here now. What is wrong, are you hurt?" he asked as he entered the structure. As soon as she saw him she threw herself into his arms.

"I'm so glad it's you," she said her body shivering with fear. "I thought it was that thing come back to get me."

"What thing?" asked John looking around to make sure he didn't miss something. "What are you talking about?"

"I was so afraid," is all she could say.

"Come over here and sit and relax," said John taking her over to the bed. "There is nothing to worry about. I'm here now. I have my bow handy. Nothing is going to hurt you. Trust me."

"It was so terrifying," was all that she could say.

"What was terrifying?" asked John.

"The thing came near where I was starting the fire. It smelled something on the metal grill. I couldn't move fast enough to get the bow and arrow. I couldn't even get my cane or crutches. I wanted the cane so I could protect myself."

"But what was it?" asked John again.

"I don't know," answered Lora starting to shake again.

"Just describe it to me," asked John. "What did it look like?"

"It looked like a big dog," she said. "But it howled at me as I crawled to the back of the house. It was a good thing that I had just lit the fire. I had just returned from the lake to get a fish you left for me in the water. The fire flared up and I think it scared it and it left. When I heard you coming I thought that it was coming back."

"That does it," said John with determination in his voice. "I will not leave you until you are ready to defend yourself or are able to come with me." John then went to the rock where he marked the days. "This morning was the 29th day since I took care of your leg and arm. That means that you have been wearing it for about four week. You need to wear it for two more weeks. I will not leave you for more than a few hours and not far from here.

"Oh, Johnny," she said apologetically. "I'm so sorry to have been such a drag."

"You're not a drag," said John. "Don't you understand that I love you? Another thing," said John now deep in thought. "I got to close this place up. I need to make a wall for the open side. I also need to make a door for the door way."

"That's a good idea," said Lora almost fully recovered. "We both might be in danger while we sleep."

"We can have a fire going all night until I close us in,"

"Anyway," said Lora. "I have the fish there in the bowl ready to cook. Do you want to cook it?"

"I also have two nice slices of deer meat. I did get a nice deer for us. It is large enough to last us for a while. I should have the work done by then. Once in a while I can catch us a fish to break the monotony." John, using the string, measured the openings he was going to close. He then went out into the woods to find small logs and strong vines to use in closing the openings. The small trees were easy, but getting the strong vine took him two days and farther from Lora that he wanted. After a week of gathering and cutting the trees he started in the construction. He bound the trees using the vines and the string as needed, at the top, the middle and the bottom. He made the end opening wall first. It would be the easiest and would give him some experience that he would need for the door. Holding the wall in place at the bottom was easy. He got several large stones to do that. The top at the right side he tied to the pole. The left side against the rock was more difficult. He had to puncture two holes in the wing, one at the end and one in the middle. That was difficult because of the lack of tools. He used a large bolt in what was left of the aircraft wreckage and after pounding it at the top of the wing it finally punctured through. It took him two days, a little at a time, to puncture the two holes. He then tied the wall tightly to the wing. His next project was the door. Making the door was the easiest. It was like making the wall. However attaching it was the problem. He sat and contemplated the different possibilities. Should it swing open like a regular door or should it swing up and be held up when open with a pole. Its weight could be balanced with a rock for leverage. He remembered how Tarzan did it in one of the movies he had seen. That would not be easy, and would require puncturing two more holes in the wing. He could attach the door to the pole with pieces of vine or double string and have it swing out as a regular door. But the weight was the problem. Its weight would rest on the ground and the door would have to be lifted or dragged on the rough ground to open or close. He decided that he would make it open as a regular door. He would solve the ground problem by finding some smooth rock for the door to slide on. That was easier to say than to do. It took him two days to find the rocks that were large enough and flat on top to do the job. It took several days for John to install the rock floor where the door would be dragging. He had to dig deeper for some holes for the rock, so that they would lay flat. He placed one at each end of the door where it would be moving. It took a little force but Lora had no problem. He pounded a stake just inside the building and attached a vine to the door so that the vines could be placed over the stake to hold the door closed.

"Now then," said John, "you are safe from any animal that comes this way."

"Thanks," said Lora. "I feel safest when you are around. But I understand that you have things to do to keep us alive."

They both settled in and after a great dinner they fell asleep feeling safe in their closed abode. John felt like sleeping for a week. He fell asleep worrying about who he now completely felt were his daughters.

John stayed around for the next couple of days. He had caught another deer and a few rabbits in between. And with catching a few fished now and then they had enough food for quite a while. John checked the stone wall for the number of days that have passed since the crash. He counted 47 days. That was more than six weeks.

"Lora, honey," he said. "Do you know that it has been over six week since I bandaged your arm and leg?"

"Are you ready to remove these awful things you have on me she asked with Joy?"

"I am if you are," responded John.

"Are you kidding, am I," she said. John started to first unravel the leg gauze. Her leg was still white from not seeing any light. He then took the tape and metal from her arm. It also looked white and shriveled. She immediately started to flex them both. It took a couple of days and she was active like a new person. To John she was back to normal although he admitted to her that he didn't know what that was. The only time he saw her walking was when they got off the plane in Chicago. They were now both very happy.

The next day John decided to go up the mountain as he had planned weeks ago to find goats.

"Go," said Lora. "Get that trip over with. I will be fine. I have plenty of food. I'll practice with the bow and arrow and will be able to protect myself. Go."

"It will take me about an hour to get there, an hour or so to climb up, an hour to look around, an hour to get down and an hour to come home. That is about five hours. It is now about nine. I should be home by about two this afternoon. He then left and as he had guessed he got there a little before ten. It took more than an hour to climb the mountain. He had to search for ways to climb to the less rocky part of the mountain. After looking around he determined that there were no animals of any kind up there. He slowly came down the mountain and got back to his living area at about three that afternoon. He looked around but couldn't see Lora anywhere. Lora was gone from the area. He decided to climb up the rock to where the help sign was to see if he could see her from there. He looked around but couldn't see her. He became very concerned. Suddenly he heard her yell from behind him.

"Johnny," she yelled. "Come up here quickly." John looked up and saw her up on the rocky area above him.

"Lora," he yelled back. "What is the matter? Do you need help? What are you doing up there anyway?"

"No, come up here," she yelled back. John could hardly make out what she was saying. He hurried up to where she was.

"What's the matter? What are you doing up here"

"Just look down there," she said pointing to an area across toward the river. "What do you see? There next to that clearing just off the river." John looked at the direction she was pointing. At first he didn't see what she was talking about. "Doesn't that look like a roof, there next to that large cliff on the right?"

"Yes," said John in amazement. It looks like asphalt roofing. It looks like some kind of a structure. Perhaps it's a house or cottage of some kind."

"Let's go see," said Lora very excitingly. "Maybe there are people down there."

"Settle down first," said John. We have to be careful going down. We don't want an accident before we get there. Remember you are getting over a broken arm and leg."

"I'm back to normal and remember I'm younger that you." That brought a smile on John's face.

"I hear you," said John. They made it down safely. Lora got excited again.

Let's go see if there are people there." She insisted.

"It's passed three-thirty," said John. "That looks like it is very far away."

"I don't care," she said. "Please let's go now." John couldn't say no seeing how excited she was. They started toward the mountain just south of their location in the direction they thought it would be. A few minutes later they got to the woods that would lead them to the clearing.

"That's what I was afraid of," said John. "This is the area I came to before, looking for deer. We can't go through here. The woods are full of barberry. We would be torn apart trying to go through here."

"What can we do?" asked Lora sounding very disappointed.

We can't go up the mountain in this area because it is very steep and are surrounded with steep cliffs," said John."I remember that the clearing is next to the river. Tomorrow we will get up early. Take some food with us and try to get there by following the river. It is too far to attempt it tonight and would be treacherous at night. Before they went to bed John rigged up two backpacks using the plastic bags and the string he had. He also tied the arrow sack on the right side of each backpack. He wasn't going anyplace without proper protection. He then went to sleep. To Lora the hours dragged till morning. The next day they got up early, with bow and arrows, and their backpacks loaded with what they felt they would need, including a bag of food. They set out through the field toward the river. A new and exciting adventure was building before them.

CHAPTER SEVEN

A new Home

THE EARLY MORNING AIR WAS still chilly. There was a slight mist in the air. As they rounded the wooded area and started down the field, a loud roar startled them. Lora was several feet ahead of John. She wanted to run back to John but the animal was between them. She would be running right into the animal's path. John had his bow and arrow read to shoot before he even realized it. The animal was behind a tree and made a small target. The animal was gray in color and very large in size. John thought that it could be a large dog. He felt it couldn't be a wolf because he understood that they generally traveled in packs.

"Lora," he yelled. "He is too small a target for me. We need to get him out and turn toward you. So make a lot of noise and run like a scared rabbit" Lora had no trouble doing both. As she did that the animal turned toward her and started out. It was a perfect target for John and his arrow found its mark on the stomach. The animal fell on its front knees. Then in anger he got up and headed towards John. John's next arrow found its way into its throat. At first it stopped and with its front paws it tried to remove the arrow. Then with a sudden burst of energy it fled down the field towards the lake and disappeared. Lora turned and after realizing that they were safe she ran back to John and almost knocked him over as she threw herself into his arms. After a few minutes to recover she pulled back and kissed John.

"You're my hero" she explained and kissed him again.

"We were lucky that it decided to chase you. You have to thank God not me," answered John.

"What in the world was it," asked Lora.

"I don't know," answered John. "It was too big for a wolf, besides wolfs travel in packs. I think it was just a large dog. It wasn't a mountain lion or a bear so it had to be a dog."

"What do you think will happen to it?"

"Well I think we scared it off with the pain it felt from my arrows and headed for the lake to wash itself. I don't know if it will make it. It probably will bleed to death on the way. Anyway it won't harm us so let's get to the river." They crossed the field and reaching the river they turned left and followed the narrow river's beach. They travelled for about an hour when they came to a place where the river flowed up against a rocky area.

"What do we do here?" asked Lora.

"Well we can either climb over the rocks or take off our shoes and walk along the edge of the river," said John, almost talking to himself. "Let me check the depth of the water." He then using an arrow stuck it at the edge of the river. It went down only about six inches. "Take off your shoes and stockings and follow me." Taking off his shoes and socks he proceeded into the water, checking all along for the depth. After about two hundred feet they came back to ground. They walked for about fifteen minutes when they came to another area where the river was against a rock formation.

"Do we take off our shoes and stockings again?" asked Lora, sitting on a rock ready to take off her shoes.

"I think this time we will climb over the rocks," said John reviewing and analyzing the area. "The last place the rocks were too rugged and it was easier to go by water. I think we can climb over these rocks without a problem." They climbed over the rocks helping each other over the larger rocks. Soon they were back on the river beach. The river here took a sharp turn to the left. This meant that it would have a larger beach because the river current would flow hard on the opposite shore. They walked having confidence that they would soon be at their destination. However, it proved to be more difficult than they had imagined. As they turned the corner past a large shrub, they found that shrubs and a few trees lined the edge of the river on top of an elevated hill. John checked the depth of the water. It was too deep. They would have to travel through the water with their backpacks over their heads and duck under the low tree branches. Lora didn't say a word. She knew that John would find a way. John decided that they would have to travel inland for a distance walking around the hill. The hill went down inland so that the trees were lined at the edge of the hill. The problem was that they were at the edge of the woods that had the heavy growth of thorny barberry. John had to cut his way around the hill. He took out his Swiss knife and slowly cut the barberry around the edge of the hill. Two hours later they found their way back to the river beach. Looking ahead they became aware that their problems were not over. The river took a sharp turn to the right and this time the edge of the river was at the bottom of over a six foot cliff. John checked the depth of the river at the cliff. He couldn't touch bottom. Again they would have to go inland, but this time by also climbing the rocks. Inland the trees and barberry were tightly against the rocks. They had only two choices. Climb the rocks and see where they would lead or go back from where they came from. After a short consultation they decided to climb the rocks. The rocks were all very large. They had to help each other up and down each as they came to them. To start the climb John had to help Lora up a five foot rock to get up to the upper level of the formation. Lora helped John by grabbing his belt as he reached the top, and pulling him up. They walked around on the inland side until they were able to turn back toward the river. They went up several levels before they could start down again. It was near the south side of the rock formation that they came to a dead end. There was a cliff of about ten feet high that they had to drop down to continue towards the river beach.

"Lorrie," said John. "We are at a very important decision point."

"What is the problem?" asked Lora.

"Well we can't go up from here. It will take us back where we came from. We can't go down inland because of the barberry. We would have to fall on the barberry. It is right up to the rocks. We can go down here. However it is a dangerous ten feet drop and if we go down here we will not be able to come back up this way."

"Why is that a problem?" asked Lora. "We don't intend to come back this way do we?"

"The problem is that we may get trapped between a rock and a hard place," said John.

"What does that mean?" asked Lora

"Look at where we want to go," said John pointing south. "The river turns left again and I can't see past the high rocks. Remember the building that we saw was up against a cliff on this side of the clearing. What if we can't get past those rock and we can't go back? We would be stranded in between."

"I say let's go," said Lora. "I truly believe that God will take care of us."

"All right," said John." Throw you backpack down first. Then slide down on your stomach and let me hold on to your hands. I have to get on my stomach and lower you. It will be about a five foot drop if you just hang on to the edge of the rock. With your leg still healing I don't think it will take that kind of a drop." Lora did as John asked she first dropped her back pack and then slowly she lowered herself down the cliff. When she felt she was about to fall she grabbed Johns hands. John lowered her to the full extent of his arms. He then let go and she landed on her feet at the bottom of the cliff.

"I'm fine," said Lora anticipating the question. "How are you going to come down?"

"I think I'll go back the way we came. I can't come down this way."

"This is no time to be funny," said Lora with a big smile on her face.

"If that is true, why are you smiling?" asked John as he slid down the rock as far as he could go, holding on just with his fingers. Finally he let go and was surprised that Lora used her body to lighten the impact of his fall by trying to catch him.

"You are something else," said John as he recovered. "Were you trying to catch me? Are you alright? Did my body hurt you?"

"No," said Lora with a smile. "I love the feel of your body"

"I'm sure that there are better ways of feeling my body."

"I take what I can get," said Lora now laughing hard.

"Let quit this foolishness and see if we can get through to the clearing." said John with a red face. They walked to the river's edge and found a narrow beach they could walk on. After what seemed like a mile they came to the rock edge that John had feared. They climbed the first rock and found that they could climb to the edge of the river by the clearing. They could now see the house to their left. The rock cliff grew higher toward the house but at the edge of the river it was only about six feet high. After dropping down the ten foot cliff this was child play. They soon were down at the edge of the clearing by the river. The grass in the clearing was knee high. Lora ran toward the house with great joyfulness. The clearing was about a little over an acre of land. The first thing that they came to before the house was a tool shed. Between the tool shed and the house there was a space of about fifty feet. That area was loaded with fire wood to about six feet high and six feet deep. Lora flew past these and reached the house. As she got there she stopped to knock on the door. When no one answered she went inside. The door was apparently unlocked. John stopped at the shed. He opened the door and went inside. He was surprised at what he saw. The shed was loaded with tools. There was a push type lawn mower and a large wheelbarrow. There also was a regular short handle sickle and next to it was a long handle sickle where the handle was at a ninety degree angle from the sickle. John had never seen a long handle one. Not being a farmer he was unsure of what it was. However he was already thinking of how he was going to use it. There also were all kinds of common digging and planting tools. Next to a shovel in the corner were a long handle ax and a large saw. He surely could have used that when he made the HELP sigh. He also was surprised to see a mattock, which he thought were only used by European old timers. It was his father's replacement for a hoe. On the wall he also found two real bows and two arrow pouches filled with arrows. On the other corner was a fishing rod and a tackle box full of fish hooks. On a shelf on the left side of the shed he found a small box full of vegetable seeds. That excited him most because it indicated that somewhere they had a garden. The only thing that John couldn't understand was the rings tied to the wall on the front of the shed and on the wall inside next to the door. It was on the left side of the building where the front wall was only about two feet wide. Under it were two boxes against the wall, one was lined inside with a metal lining. John decided he would figure it out later. For now he had a lot of work to do. He took the scythe, which he thought was a long handle sickle, and with easy sweeps he cut the grass up to the house. When he got to the house Lora came to the door.

"This is a gift from God," she said. "It has four rooms, two bed rooms, a kitchen, and a family room. The only thing it doesn't have is a bath room."

"If you look past the house by the trees you will find what you are looking for, an outhouse."

"I have a lot cleaning to do before we can move in. What are your plans for today?"

"I think I better clear the barberry from the woods to our old home," said John.

"That's good thinking," said Lora. "If any one sees our sign we need to be able to get there and direct them, besides we need to get the deer."

"You know, you never cease to amaze me," said John. "You are a very intelligent woman. You are right up there with what is going on and what is important."

"Do you want to eat before you start working?"

"No, I had better get to work, besides we don't have that much food with us. It would be great for this evening when I come back tired and hungry."

"Whatever you say," said Lora. "By the way, where did you get the scythe?"

"You know what this is?" asked John being surprised. "You're not from the farms so how do you know what this is?"

"I don't know," said Lora. "I must have seen one in the old movies."

"There are many such tools in the shed. I will tell you about them when we eat tonight. See you later," he said. Shaking his head John started to walk away.

"Before you go," said Lora. "Would you mind clearing a path to the river with your scythe? I have a lot of washing to do and it would be difficult dragging everything through the tall grass. Also I suggest you take a bow and arrow with you."

"I'll be glad to," said John as he started back clearing a path to the river. On the way back he stopped at the shed and grabbed the bow and arrow. That was a good suggestion he thought. He then cleared a path to the woods and started to clear the barberry from the obvious previous path through the woods. He found it easier than he had believed. The barberry in the path was newer than the barberry in the woods that he had cut getting to the house. Where it was harder he cut it higher. He would have to come back anyway with the mattock to remove the roots. He didn't want the barberry to grow back any time soon. Slowly he worked down the path. Time went by unnoticed by John. He was too busy working.

"Johnny," yelled Lora. "Come and eat. It is dusk and will be dark soon." John hadn't noticed because it was dark in the woods anyway and it got darker the farther he went in. He set the mattock against a tree besides the bow and arrows he had set there earlier and looked back at where the house was. Although it was dusk he could see white bed sheets hanging from a rope that was connected between the shed and the house. He noticed that there were also bed spreads and pillow covers. As he started to walk back he realized how tired he was. He walked slowly to the house. Lora was taking in the things she had hanged to dry. They were already dry. As John got there Lora was talking.

"These will do for now," she said as she pulled in the pillow covers. "We will use the ships pillows when we get to the old shelter." John went in with her and sat at the table where Lora had warmed the food they had brought with them.

"Lora, you can't believe how tired I am. I guess I'm out of shape and not used to hard work."

"I'm not in the least surprised," said Lora. "You have been out there since about two-thirty. You have been working for over five hours. On top of that you were working on an empty stomach. Get something to eat and we will go to sleep early. I'm kind of beat myself. I have washed all four floors and the bed sheets and all the other linen plus the kitchen ware."

"Earlier you asked about the tools I found in the shed. I can't believe what they brought up here," said John ignoring her statement. "There is a hand lawn mower, a wheelbarrow, two powerful looking bows with arrows, some fishing gear, and most important some vegetable seeds."

"Vegetable seed?" said Lora. "What would they do with them?"

"I think that some where they had a garden," said John.

"I guess that makes sense, but where?"

"We don't have time to look now," said John. "We have to finish the path through the woods first."

"You're right of course, but we have to do it soon if we are to plant them," added Lora. After some small talk they went to bed. They were both dead tired.

The next morning John got up early. He got dressed, drank some water and left without bothering Lora who was asleep in the other bedroom. He went down the path he had cleared the day before and found that nothing had been disturbed. He went immediately to work clearing the rest of the path. It was around noon that he heard Lora yelling for him. He put down his equipment as he had done the night before and headed back to the house.

"Johnny," she yelled thinking he had not heard her. "Would you like some chicken soup for lunch?" John heard her and became angry. He was sure she didn't have chicken soup. It was a bad joke, he thought. When he came to the clearing he yelled back at her.

"That's not only a bad joke, but it's in very poor taste," he yelled.

"Who is joking?" she yelled back. "It's a simple question. Do you want some chicken soup?" John was too tired to argue with her. It would be their first fight. He was still unhappy with her sense of humor. When he got to the house he gave her a very unhappy look. "Oh Johnny," said Lora. "Do you think I could be that cruel?" John was about to answer when he looked at the table. He was shocked. There on the table were two bowls with something in them that looked two thick to be just water. Alone side of each bowl were pieces that looked like bread crusts.

"What is this?" said John in a haze. "Where did you get whatever it is?"

"Johnny, it is chicken soup. Sit down and eat. I'll explain everything to you." John took a spoon full of the soup and turned to Lora.

"Honey, this is really chicken soup. How, where," was all he could say. Then, feeling bad at his anger he added, "Honey I'm so sorry to have doubted you. Can you ever forgive me?"

"There is nothing to forgive," responded Lora. "I only meant to surprise you. I probably handled it all wrong."

"Well you certainly did surprise me," said John with a smile. "What is this other stuff?"

"It is some flower I found but there is no yeast so I made bread without it. It is unleavened bread I think the Jews called it. Let me tell you of my day. I washed the floor, all the utensils and started looking around the kitchen when I saw this knob in the wall next to the cabinets. I pulled on it and found a pantry. It was full of cans of different kinds of vegetables and several kinds of canned soup. I think there are about twenty or thirty cans. In there I also found a sack of flower. I removed the top layer which looked a little moldy and baked the bread. I'm not finished reviewing the contents of the pantry."

"Well I had better get back to work. I think I can finish it by tonight. Then I can take the wheelbarrow and get some deer meat. Or do you have something else up your sleeve for dinner tonight."

"Nothing but some warm vegetables from a can," answered Lora. With a big smile John kissed her and left to finish the path. It was about two hours later that Lora came up to him in the path.

"Johnny," she started. "I think I know where the garden was. I was looking around the clearing when I came to an area about twenty feet by twenty feet that was different from the other section of the clearing. It was the only place that didn't have grass. We didn't notice it because it is also very green, but it isn't grass. It's full of weeds. That's where the garden must have been. Also, all around it there is an aluminum edge that keeps the grass out. We couldn't see it because of the tall grass."

"What kind of weeds is growing there?" asked John.

"I think that most of it dandelions," said Lora.

"Did the dandelions have flowered yet?" asked John getting all excited.

"No," answered Lora. "I think that there are small buds on some of them but no flowers. Why do you ask?"

"Oh Lora," said John showing his excitement. "Don't you know what you have found? It is the vegetable we will have tonight. The only wild food better is Lucia. It has many names. In Italian it is call Chicoria. Also I think it has the American name of Chicory."

"How do I cook it?" asked Lora.

"You just cut in down at the roots and boil it until tender."

"Great, I'll go cook it for tonight if you bring some meat. Actually the reason I came down here is to ask you if you wanted me to dig it up while you are clearing the path."

"No," said John. "I will do that later. You have plenty of work making this place home. Besides, if the area is full of dandelions we don't want to dig it all out. We will plant as we eat the dandelions. Pick the dandelions from one end so that we could start planting as we eat up the dandelions."

"Sounds like a plan," said Lora and started back to the house. John continued his work and by late afternoon he was through to the clearing near their old shelter. He decided to hold off on clearing the roots in the path. Getting food and the supplies they had left behind was more important. He was sure that he would have no trouble getting through with the wheel barrow. Making that decision he returned to the shed and got the wheelbarrow. He notified Lora of his plans as he passed the house and headed down the path. When he got to the clearing he preceded passed their old shelter through the north field to the river where the deer meat was stored in the cold water. He was surprised to see a large fish attached to the line they had left in the water. They had forgotten all about the fish line in their excitement of getting to the new home. He pulled the deer onto the wheelbarrow and set the fish on top and headed back to the house. When he got there he went directly to the river and attached the deer line to the dock and let the dear sink in the cold water. He returned to the house with the fish.

"You are just in time," said Lora when she saw him. "I just took some soup and the dandelion from the stove. I see that you got a fish. Where did you get that?"

"In the excitement we forgot that we had the fish hook in the river next to the deer. Anyway we have enough of a food variety for the next couple of days." After eating, John was so tired that he decided to go right to bed. When he got up to leave Lora grabbed him by the arm.

"Where are you going?" she asked.

"Lorrie, I'm so tired that I thought I would go directly to bed. It's been a very long day."

"I was hoping that we could sit on the davenport for a few minutes with your arms around me," she said with a very loving expression on her face. "Do you realize that you only kissed me once since the day before we left for here?"

"I know, sweetheart," said John apologetically. "I have not been as attentive as I should have been. OK, let's sit for a little while. I've missed having my arms around you too." He sat down and she sat next to him. He put his arms around her. "Put you head here on my shoulder and cuddle up," he said. She did as he asked. After a few minutes she turned her head towards him. He bent over and looked down at her. "You are so beautiful," he said as he kissed her. The kiss lasted longer then he thought it would. A few minutes later her tongue found its way to his mouth and cuddled with his tongue. Passion rose in both of them. They started to press their bodies together. Final, worrying that in their tired state that it might get out of hand Lora pulled away.

"You had better go to bed," said Lora. "I know you. You will get up early in the morning knowing there is a lot of work you have to do."

"Who can go to sleep now?" said John. "I'm wide awake. Let's cuddle some more."

"Only one hour per customer," she kidded him.

"How am I going to go to sleep after that?"

"You just have to lie down and cool off. You soon will go to sleep."

"You're a tough lady, you know that?" he said, although he was already half asleep.

The next morning, just as Lora predicted, John was up with the sun. He walked into the kitchen and was surprised to see that Lora was also up.

"What are you doing up so early?" he asked.

"I got up to make you breakfast," she answered. John was about to answer when he saw a steaming bowl setting on the table.

"What is this you concocted now?" he asked.

"It's a bowl of Mother's Oats," she responded.

"I'm afraid to ask where you got it," he responded.

"I was checking the pantry to see how many cans of food we had. I could see some cans on the top shelf but it was too high for me to see behind them. So I got a chair to stand on and checked the top shelf. Behind the cans I found four boxes. There was a box of Mother's Oats, a box of farina, a box of Cheerios, and a box of salt. We can now salt our food that has tasted so bland. Oh, and I found a large can of coffee. Tomorrow you will have some farina and a cup of coffee.

"You are amazing," said John in a state of stupor. After eating he thanked her with several kisses, and headed for the shed. He grabbed the wheelbarrow and headed for the old shelter. He grabbed everything that they had left there. Most important was the medical box, the pillows and the blankets. He then headed back to the house. When he got there Lora was up and cleaning the areas of the house she had not cleaned.

"Oh good," she said. "I was hoping you would bring everything from the old shelter. After she brought everything inside, John headed back to the shed. He grabbed the maddox and was soon pulling out the barberry roots. It was easier then he thought it would be. It only took one swing with the maddox to get each root out. The maddox would dig deep under the root and it came out when John pulled on the maddox. John had seen his father us one but had never used one himself. It was a little after noon when Lora called him to lunch.

"You have to keep your health up," she said when he showed up. John was shocked when he got there and saw what was hanging on the clothes line. There were three pairs of jeans three blue work shirts and a woman's blouse.

"Where did these come from?" asked John still in a state of shock.

"I was cleaning out the closets and found them there. Two of the jeans are male jeans. One pair is size forty and the other is size thirty-eight. They must have had on older son with them. The other jeans are woman's jeans and fit me perfectly. I also found a large medical kit. It has everything we would ever need. It has a large supply of gauze. Anyway before you go back to work try them on. Leave me you old clothes so I can wash them. Besides you don't want to continue working in your good clothes. Also leave me your underwear so I can wash them too. You can work without them for a little while." John did as she suggested. He came back out of his bedroom wearing a pair of the jeans and one of the blue shirts.

"Both jeans fit me," John informed Lora. "The forty fit me kind of loose and these that I am wearing fit snugly."

"Great," said Lora. "Now come eat your lunch." She had a can of soup and some unleavened bread ready for him. John ate and soon was back digging the roots. It was a little passed three when he finished pulling out the roots. Then using the maddox on its side, using it as a rake, he leveled the area all the way back to the clearing. Since it was still early he exchanges the maddox for the scythe and cut all the grass in the clearing and especially around the garden area. He noticed that Lora had cleared about a fourth of the area by pulling out the dandelions. He now knew what vegetable he was going to have for dinner. He had cut the grass down low enough so that the lawn mower could now cut it down to the normal height. However, before he could do that, he had to remove the long grass cuttings. He got a rake from the shed and racked the grass into a large pile and set it on the far corner of the clearing next to the woods. Little did he know how handy that pile would become? As he was ready to leave he noticed that where Lora had pulled the dandelions some earth worms were showing up. John grabbed a large one and getting the fishing hooks and a line he set the worm on the hook and placed it in the water. He then returned to the house. As he approached the house he noticed that all his clothes and Lora clothes including both their underclothes were drying on the clothes line. When he got within hearing range, Lora shouted out to him.

"John will you get a couple of slices of deer please," she asked.

"How about a couple of rib steaks? John resounded" That evening they ate the deer and were ready to repeat last night's action.

The next day, John got up early as usual, had his farina, and using the lawn mower, he finished mowing the entire clearing. He then grabbed the maddox and started to dig up the garden area. He dug up almost a third of the area picking some dandelions to make room. When he was finished he went in for lunch. He explained to Lora what he had accomplished.

"We now have to decide what vegetables we have to plant first. We can plan the ones that we think will grow fastest after we have consumed the remainder of the dandelions.

"I don't know much about vegetable gardens," said Lora. "I imagine that things like tomatoes take the longest. Everything I can tell you will be my best guess."

"It's the same with me," agreed John. "Let's us confer together and come up with the best guess.

"I think that anything that has a fruit will take longer," said Lora.

"That's good thinking," said John. "I agree completely. So let's list them.

"Tomato is my first choice," said Lora. "My second choice would be zucchini."

"Great," said John." What do you think of string beans as the next choice?"

"That about covers the seeds we have for anything that has a fruit," said Lora. "All that is left that we have seeds for are Swiss chard, lettuce, and broccoli. After lunch John started to walk away.

"I think broccoli should be next. It is kind of a fruit. I'll start planting them right away," said John.

"Wait, "said Lora. "That could wait for a few hours. I need you to do something for me."

"What do you need?" asked John.

"I need you to go to your bedroom and rest until I get back," said Lora not really knowing how to ask him what she really wanted. 'What's going on?" Asked John not having any idea of what she was talking about.

"When you went hunting, before we moved here, I went into the river and bathed and washed my cloths several times. Here I haven't gone at all and I feel like I'm swinging in mud. I need to bathe badly."

"So what do you need from me" asked John still confused.

"I need you to be somewhere where you can't see me," she answered shyly. "I want to bathe and wash my jeans and blouse before I put on my clean underwear. I will go down to the river wearing a robe that I found in the closet."

"Now I understand," said John. "But why are you making such a big deal about it?"

"I'm shy," is all that she would answer. "I suggest that you do the same. You haven't washed since the crash, have you?" asked Lora

"I'll never tell," said John with a smile on his face. "I take it you want to go right now?"

"Yes, I should go while you eat lunch. I think a good a time for you to go is just before supper," said Lora. "I think we should do this at least once a week. I also think about six is a good time for you since it will still be bright and warm. You wouldn't want to go back to work after washing up and get dirty and sweated up again. I can't do it at that time since I have to make dinner. You should wash yourself before we eat dinner. After dinner while you wash the dishes I will wash your clothes"

"All right," said John. "Sounds like a good plan. Frankly I have wanted to do this for days." "Go ahead and do your thing." John ate his lunch and went into the bed room. It was less than an hour later when Lora came back into the house.

"John" she called out, "I'm all done. You can go back to work." As John left he could see Lora hanging her clothes on the clothes line. He went out to the garden area and using the maddox he dug three trenches where he could plant the vegetables. He was finished about five thirty and returned to the house. "Go ahead. And do your thing," said Lora. "I'll cook dinner and wait for you in my bedroom." John went into his bedroom, removed his clothes and put on the robe Lora had placed on his bed. After he had washed up he returned and they ate dinner. After dinner Lora when out and washed Johns clothes and hug them on the clothes line.

"Now don't you feel better?" asked Lora when she was through.

"Like a million dollars," responded John. "Now, come sit on the couch with me. I would like to spend the rest of the evening with my arms around you."

"You don't have to ask me twice," said Lora as she threw herself into his arms. She only got up once to get Johns clothes. They finally fell asleep in each other's arms. They were both more tired than they thought.

The next day, after eating breakfast, John planted the vegetables and after he had watered them he checked the food supply. He found that he had caught a fish but the deer meat was getting low.

"You know Lora," he said after returning to the house. "We have about another week's supply of deer meat. I think we need to go hunting."

"I'm glad you said we," responded Lora. "I'm going with you where ever you go."

"That sounds great to me," said John. "It has been very lonely hunting alone, besides the fact that I always worried about your safety."

"Did you really worry about me?"

"Always," said John with a very serious look on his face. Lora noticing his seriousness responded with a loving answer.

"I believe you because I always worried about your safety." After lunch, they packed all they needed and headed outdoors.

"I think that we should head south," said John. "I think we have scared off all the deer in this area. Let's follow the river's edge going around the south side of this area." He walked toward the river and headed south past the dock and around the rocky area across from the house, Lora followed closely behind. When they rounded the corner they came to a wooded area. Still keeping on the edge of the river they came to a clearing. The river turned east behind a rocky area.

"I wonder if we can go any farther?" asked Lora.

It looks like the whole area is at a higher level," said John. Look at both sides of the river and as far east as we can see. It looks like it's all uphill."

"I guess if we are to go further we have to climb these rocks," commented Lora. What is that noise? It sounds like there is a rapid just behind those rocks"

"I guess it could be," said John."The river is coming from a higher level. As long as we are here let's go exploring. Curiosity is in my blood. Let's climb up these rocks over to the left a little. It looks like it will be a little easier to climb." They proceeded across the field heading east to the area that looked to be easier to climb. It took them several minutes to get to the top of the hill.

"You were right," said Lora in astonishment. "The whole area is at a higher level. It's like this is the correct level and we just climbed out of a hole."

"It is very strange isn't it?" said John. Lora then decided to walk west toward the river. Her curiosity about the strange noise got to her. When she got to the edge of the area she looked down at the river.

"Johnny," she yelled very excitingly. "Come see this. It's the most beautiful sight I've seen in a long time." John rushed over to where Lora was standing and looked at what Lora was viewing.

"Wow," is all that John could say. "That is very beautiful. So the noise we heard was not a rapids but a very beautiful water fall."

"How high do you think it is?" asked Lora.

"It looks like it's about a twenty to thirty feet water fall," said John. "I think it is about as high as we have climbed up to this level. Maybe it's about three feet shorter. Look how the river is rushing down to the falls. It's winding like a snake through the mountains."

"It's so beautiful and relaxing watching it," said Lora. "I feel like I don't ever want to leave. I could just sit on this rock and stay here forever."

"You would soon starve to death," said John with a grin on his face. "Anyway we had better leave and go find some food."

"I know," said Lora. "I'm just expressing what I feel." They started down the way they came. When they got to the bottom, they were about to cross the field when Lora grabbed John by the arm and pulled him behind a rock. Before John knew what was happening he saw Lora fire an arrow towards the woods. His automatic reaction had an arrow on his bow and ready to fire. Lora had spotted a deer and her arrow caught it in the neck. John's arrow followed soon after and his arrow pierced the deer in the belly. They rushed over to the deer. It was kicking a little but it was dead.

"You never fail to amaze me," said John. "You're faster that a Cheetah. I will never stop admiring you."

"I'm just hungry," said Lora with a smirk on her face. They dragged it as far as they could to the clearing by the dock. There they dressed it and slipped it into the water where they had the other deer. They cut some meat from the old deer and prepared it for dinner.

"You know," said John almost to himself. "We should go back, but this time go up the gradual slope on the far left of where we went up. I notice that the area there not only has a gentle slope but I notice that it had a lot of shrubs and green growth. I think that it would support a lot of rabbits and deer." Lora was too busy preparing dinner. After dinner John repeated what he has said about their next trip. "It will be some time before our vegetable garden gives us any produce. "I think we should also go back to see if any of that growth has anything we could eat. Perhaps it has nothing more than more dandelions."

"There are no more dandelions in the garden?" asked Lora, not having been to the garden area.

"No," responded John, "I picked the last when I planted the Swiss chard, the lettuce and the broccoli."

"I guess we can go tomorrow," said Lora. "We now have enough food for a while. We can go and investigate that end of the mountain."

"There is another thing that became obvious to me. I don't know if you have thought of this but it's important."

"What are you talking about," asked Lora.

"Well," said John. "Have you thought of the fact that no boat could come down or go up over the falls? That means that the people who built this house had to come from the north. That means that they must have come from perhaps as far as Canada.

"Do you really think we are near Canada?" asked Lora.

"I don't really know," said John. "I figured that we were about half way to Denver when the pilot turned north to escape the storm. However I figure that the storm was coming from the north heading south east. It was moving toward us, so the no way was the pilot going to go around it. The winds from the storm would be pushing us east. So if we were in Nebraska when he turned north, and the plane was going between five hundred and six hundred miles an hour, then we would have traveled between five hundred and six hundred miles. That would take us to North Dakota or Canada."

"I wish I hadn't asked," said Lora.

"I was just saying that they had to come from the north. Probably as far as Canada"

"Why is that important to me?" asked Lora.

"Well perhaps if we go north down the river we could possibly meet other camps or a small city. This river may even go into a larger river like the Missouri river."

"So maybe we should go there first," said Lora. "We have lots of food, the garden needs more time, so now is the perfect time to go."

"Spoken like the sharp minded lovable Lorrie that I know and love," said John. "So you're telling me that I had better start building a raft."

"That, using your Swiss knife will take you a week to cut down the number of trees you will need," said Lora sadly.

"Not at all," said John. "Didn't I tell you that in the shed I found a large saw? It shouldn't take me more than a day."

"It's too late now. Why don't you start tomorrow morning and we will plan on leaving the next day," suggest Lora. "While you are doing that, I will get our back packs and everything we will need ready to travel."

"Sounds like a good plan," said John. "We can leave early and plan to stay overnight one evening. We will go down the river and paddle over to the north side of the lake. We can then walk north until evening. We will sleep there and if we don't find anything we can come back to the lake and paddle to the south side of the lake from where we can walk home." They ate dinner and went to bed early dreaming of the new adventure that they would be experiencing soon.

CHAPTER EIGHT

Days of Hope

JOHN GOT UP EARLY. HE made some coffee and left for the shed. He grabbed the saw and a spool of rope and set them in front of the shed where he could get them when he was ready to leave. He returned to the house and found Lora had made some Mother's Oats.

"You have a lot of work to do," she said. "So you need a good breakfast. Also thanks for making the coffee. I was surprised to see it on the stove when I got up. You make a good cup of java."

"Thank you," said John as he sat down to eat his breakfast. "I didn't want to wake you so I made coffee. That was all I was going to have before I left. So thank you for the breakfast." John quickly ate the food drank the coffee and after kissing Lora he got up to leave.

"You have a good day," said Lora "And remember we don't have to leave tomorrow."

"I shouldn't have too much trouble getting done today," said John.

"Are you kidding me?" said Lora. "You have a lot of wood to cut."

"I don't think it will be too hard," said John. "With the large wood saw I found in the shed, cutting trees will not be the big problem. The big problem will be finding small straight trees."

"That's a break," said Lora. "God is always looking out for us." John then left, picked up the saw and rope, and headed south around the big rock next to the river across from the house. It was in that area, before they got to the falls, that John had noticed younger trees. He was hoping that there he could find sufficient smaller straight trees to build the platform for them to ride on. Getting large trees for the floating main structure would be easy. He figured that he would only need two to support the platform if he didn't get too thick platform trees. He stood awhile figuring what he would need. He realized that he should have done this the night before to save time this morning. He figured that the raft should be about five feet wide and six feet long. By picking platform trees about three inches in diameter, for six feet he would need six times four, or twenty four trees, at five feet long. He felt that thicker trees would add too much weight and he would need a stronger base. He settled on three inches. He was sure he would have no trouble finding three inch trees. By ten he had cut down two large trees for the base and twelve three inch trees for the platform. He placed the larger logs perpendicular to the river and then tied the smaller logs together as he cut them to size, and set them cross wise on the larger logs. That covered about half of the platform he needed. Finding twelve more was going to be a problem. After he searched for two hours he was able to get four more logs for the platform by cutting branches from larger trees. After tying them in place he was still short eight logs. Since it was almost noon he decided to go home for lunch and search for the other needed logs in the other woods near the old shelter he had built. He was surprised when he got home that Lora had a hot lunch ready for him.

"How did you know that I was even coming home for lunch besides knowing the exact hour?" said John.

"Don't you know how much I love you?" she answered.

"I love you too," said John, "but what does that have to do with anything?"

"Well, through my love you have become a part of me," she answered as she kissed him. The kiss lasted long enough that John forgot what they were talking about. After eating John grabbed the wheelbarrow and headed for the woods north of the old shelter. The woods there were much larger and it was easy for John to find four trees that would provide four of the logs he need. He stopped at four because four was the most John could carry in the wheelbarrow. He soon had the logs back to the river where he was building the raft. He tied them in place and headed back to the woods for the other four he needed. It was almost six when he finished the raft. From a large tree he cut off a piece of bark as flat as he could get. It was about the size of a shovel. He found a branch that could make a good pole. He split the bottom of the pole and fastened the bark to it. It would make a great paddle. He tied a long rope to the front of the raft with one end of the rope on one side and the other end of the rope on the other side. He pulled it down the river and tied it to the dock by the house. Lora had dinner ready and after they ate they sat down and discussed what they would need for the trip.

"I found three real backpacks in the shed," said Lora. "They were hidden down behind the large box at the far end of the shed"

"That's great," said John. "I was wondering how we were going to carry all the stuff we will need. It looks like there is plenty of room in them."

"It has a nice place to put a blanket and a place for arrows built into the side," said Lora. "I have two of the packs nearly packed. I have placed in each pack, four cans of soup. Also while you were building the raft, I went to the old shelter you built, and picked up the wye stick and placed one in each of the packs. That's if by any chance we can get a rabbit we will be prepared to cook it without you going out and find the sticks you need."

"You think of everything don't you?" said John in admiration. "Have you packed any cloths?"

"Yes," said Lora with a contended look on her face. "I put an extra pair of pants, two Tee Shirts I found in the back closet, a regular shirt in your pack. I also put all that I will need in my back pack."

"I guess we are ready to travel early tomorrow morning," said John. "As soon as we get up have a good breakfast and get going by eight."

"I'll make some pan cakes and some hot coffee," said Lora. "We will need a good breakfast because we don't know what or when we will eat again."

"Sounds like we are ready," said John. "Now we should relax for the rest of the evening in each other's arms."

"Sounds like a great plan said Lora as she cuddled up in John's arms on the couch. After much passionate kissing they both fell asleep in each other's arms. They didn't wake until after one and sleepily they each went to their own bedroom.

The next morning they got up at eight. They were both very excited about their trip. They ate breakfast and taking care of last minute details they climbed onto the raft. John unhooked it from the dock and the river slowly moved them down stream. Using the paddle he had made he kept the raft near the far side of the river.

"I'll try to keep the raft near the far side of the river," said John. "You don't know what we could find on that side, especially where the river gets pretty wide downstream"

"I had the same thought," said Lora. "I have been concentrating on looking on that side." They drifted down the river in silence looking for some possible signs of life. About a half hour later they reach a point where the river turned east.

"It's amazing," said John. "There is absolutely no sign of man ever being here. You would expect to see burned out logs from a bond fire, at least one along the river. But there is nothing."

"I see a small stream that is flowing into this river," said Lora

""Yes," responded John. "I saw one a few minutes ago. They are all coming from the western mountains."

"How far into the wilderness are we?" asked Lora. "How did that house we are living in come to be there?"

"We really don't know where we are," said John. "That house may have been built by someone who wanted to be as far as they could from society. Perhaps it was built by someone trying to get away from the law."

"Would he take his wife and son with him?" asked Lora.

"Why not," said John. "If they loved him they would want to be with him."

"I don't think so," said Lora in rebuttal. "They had to make many trips to get everything up here."

"You make a good point," said John in agreement. "Let's concentrate as to where we are going."

"I don't think we know exactly where we are going," said Lora with a small chuckle." John smiled at her but didn't answer. Soon they could see the lake ahead of them. As they got closer they wondered what the transition to the lake would be like. From where they were it seemed like the lake was a little lower than the river. John wondered if there was a water fall. As they got closer even Lora noticed the difference in the water levels.

"Is there a big waterfall ahead of us?" she asked.

"I don't think it is too big," said John. "I hope we can get over it without trouble. One thing is for sure, we will not be able to go back that way." As they got near the edge John kept the raft as close to the land as possible.

"What are your thoughts?" asked Lora seeing how he was so close to the land.

"I want to be close to the land so that if the falls is too high we can get off before we go over the falls." It was hard to see from the top of the falls how high the falls really was. As they got almost to the edge of the falls, John decided that they could survive going over. He had determined that they will take the chance.

"I have decided that we are going over the falls," said John. "So, put on your backpack and grab one of the rope ends that tie the platform logs together and hang on." They had taken their backpacks off when they first got on the raft. They quickly put them on and grabbed a rope end near the center of the raft. They no sooner put them on when the raft plunged over the falls. They were both thrust backwards when the raft tilled over the falls and then thrust forward when the raft hit the water in the lake. They both hung on and soon they were moving very slowly across the lake.

"Are you all right?" asked John.

"Yes," said Lora. "It wasn't as bad as I thought it would be."

"The falls was less than a foot high," said John. "What concerns me is how did they get the boat to the house we are staying in. They couldn't come down from the south and now it looks like they couldn't come from the north."

"Didn't you say that the lake changed in size between the spring and the fall?" asked Lora. "Perhaps when they came the falls was in inches."

"Or non existing," said John in admiration. "You are so special. Of course you are right. It had to be that way. There is no other answer. When we first crashed the lake was just as we see it now. However, later the lake had risen so that it covered our part of the ship. It stayed that way for quite a while. I'll bet now that our part of the ship is again out in the open. We may go down there someday. Remember there was a forest to the east of our plane section that we couldn't get to because the lake had risen so high. Perhaps now we can get to it to hunt."

"How far down the lake shall we go?" asked Lora changing the subject. "I see that we are hardly moving."

"There is only a small current in the lake." said John. "I would like to go as far as the out flowing river. We can tie the raft there. We will need it to get back across the lake so that we can walk home from there."

"Can't we go some distance down the river," asked Lora.

"No because the flow is too strong and we will not be able to come back to the lake. Then we will not be able to cross the lake unless you want to swim across the lake which is over a thousand foot swim. Even if you could swim that distance would you like to swim over a couple hundred dead bodies," said John kidding her.

"Let's get off here," said Lora with a smirk.

"Soon," said John. As they got close to the river John noticed that the flow got stronger and so he decided that they were close enough. With the paddle he pushed the raft toward the shore. When he got close Lora who had realized what John was doing jumped off the raft, grabbed the rope and started to pull the raft to the shore. John jumped over right after her, grabbed the other end of the rope and together they pulled the raft on shore.

"Let's pull it as far as we can so that nothing will pull it back into the lake," said John. However, when the raft was completely out of water it became very heavy. They couldn't pull it inland any farther.

"That's the best we can do," said Lora. "I'm exhausted." John grabbed the raft's rope and taking it to the nearest tree tied it firmly. He didn't want to swim across the lake either. It was about nine-thirty when they left the raft.

"It looks like the river from here north is pretty wide and we have plenty of shore to walk on." said John. "The river also seems pretty straight. I don't think we have many rocks to climb." They started to walk north down the river. As they walked they could see more of the river but it looked like more of the same. It was about twelve o'clock when they stopped to rest.

"It seems like we haven't gone anywhere," said Lora as she sat down and started to take out the sandwiches she had prepared for the journey.

"Good Idea," said John. "Let's rest here and eat the sandwiches before they go bad in this heat."

"How much farther do you think we should go?" said Lora. "I don't see that we are gaining anything from this trip."

"That may seem true but I think we should continue until we decide to spend the night. If we don't get any other ideas we will start back the next morning. What I would like to do is climb that mountain there by the river's edge a few miles down the river from here and look north down the river as far as we can see."

"That doesn't seem that far away," said Lora. "We should make it in a couple hours."

"Don't be fooled, said John. "Mountains are always farther away then they seem." They finished their lunch and started down the river. After they walked a couple of hours, Lora sat down on a rock to rest. The way was not difficult but going around trees and grass from time to time it did get tiresome.

"This is a strange trip," said Lora. "It seems to alternate between nice river sand, trees, and high grass. And what is stranger then all is that the mountain you want to climb seems to be moving away from us."

"I told you," said John with a giggle in his voice. "It does seem to be moving farther away as we approach it. It's an optical elution. However we are gaining on it." After a five minute rest they continued down the river. It was about six in the evening when they arrived at the foot of the mountain.

"We have been walking for over eight hours," said Lora. "I don't think we should try climbing the mountain today anymore."

"Your right," said John. "We will get an early start tomorrow. We have no idea what we will come across going to the top. We will need full daylight coming down. Let start a fire and warm some of that soap you brought. You go look for fire wood" John started to look for rocks and whatever fire wood he could find around the area close to him. Suddenly he noticed that Lora was not around where he could see her. "Lora," he yelled out. But he heard no answer. He wondered where she would go for fire wood. He thought that he should have asked her to stay close. The woods that were located just behind them should have had plenty of fire wood. After waiting about ten minutes that seemed like an hour he prepared to go looking for her. He got his bow and arrow and was ready to go when he saw her coming out of the woods. She was carrying a load of fire wood and something else. John could not tell.

"Where have you been?" asked John with a worried look on his face.

"I'm sorry I got out of sight," said Lora seeing the worried look on John's face. She was trying to get her explanation before he would get harsh with her. "I was looking for fire wood when I saw the rabbit deeper in the woods. I chased it and finally got near enough to shot it. I'm sorry," she repeated. "I'll not get out of your sight without telling you."

"I was worried about you," is all that John could say feeling out of reasons to be angry with her.

"If you are as tired as I am, I thought that a good rabbit dinner would perk us up."

"Good thinking," said John. Lora then pulled out the wye sticks from their backpacks and started to pound them into the ground with one of the stones John had placed around the fire. John stocked up the fire dressed the rabbit and placed it over the fire. Rabbit never tasted so good. After eating they talked awhile about the trip and about nine they made a bed with their blankets and were soon fast asleep in each other's arms.

The next morning Lora got up first. She placed more wood on the fire and made coffee from the river water and some coffee grinds she had in her backpack. She had hot coffee by the time John woke up.

"You are up early," said John.

"I thought we should have a hot cup of coffee before we start the big climb, said Lora. "I don't know if you noticed but the mountain looks much higher from here than it did yesterday."

"Yesterday we were several miles away," said John drinking his coffee. "We had better get going. I hope we will get there and back before lunch." After putting out the fire and getting their things together they started up the mountain. It was about eight in the morning. It was pretty easy going for the first hour, but the farther they went up the tougher the climb became. The rocks got bigger as they went up. Soon they found that they had to go around the mountain to find places that they could climb. About ten they came to a place that they could climb no further. The rock was about ten feet high.

"This looks like a dead end," said Lora. "What do we do now?"

"I see that there is a place to climb down around the other side of this rock."

"Yes," said Lora. "But how do we get there?"

I think we have to go down to the lower level so we can get to the other side."

"We have to go down before we can go up," said Lora almost to herself. They backed up and went down to a lower level. From there they were able to get to the other side of the ten foot rock. From there they climbed above the rock and proceeded up the mountain. They had to go down two other times to get farther up the mountain. It was about noon when they reached the top. They worked their way around until they were on the river side of the mountain. From there they could see many miles down the river. They explored both sides of the river from just below them to as far as they could see. There was nothing except the same thing that they had seen on the way to the mountain.

"There is absolutely no sign of any human ever being in this part of the country," said John sadly, "nothing!"

"Well at least we found out," said Lora in an attempt to cheer John up a little. She had seen the sad expression on his face. "If we hadn't come here we would be wondering if there were people close to us farther north. Now we know."

"I guess you are right," is all that John could say.

"We had better start down if we want to get down before dark," said Lora. "We don't have anything to eat except the soup, and I think we should wait until we get down the mountain."

"As if we could have the soup up here," said John. "What would we use for fire wood? I don't think either one of us would want to eat it cold." They started to climb down. It was more difficult getting down then it was getting up. Going down they had to be more careful of falling. It took almost five hours getting back down. When they finally got to the flat ground at the bottom of the hill it was passed five.

"I don't know about you," said Lora. "I'm too tired to go any farther today. Let's make a fire and eat our dinner here. We can get a fresh start in the morning."

"I'm with you," said John. "It may be the last time in a while that I can fall asleep with my arms around you."

"Very funny," said Lora. "You can put your arms around me any time you want. However, I don't want you to fall asleep." They both broke down laughing. They were both so tired that a little humor went a long way. John soon had a fire burning bright. They ate the soup and relaxed on a rock near the water. The sound of the flowing river helped them feel restful.

The next morning Lora was up first. She set more wood on the dwindling fire and made some coffee. John woke just in time for the coffee.

"You are a gift from heaven," said John as he poured himself some coffee. "Let's get started for home."

"It's funny that you said that," said Lora with a smile. "It is only a four room shack but somehow it's home to us. "I can't wait to get to my kitchen and cook you a nice tasty dinner."

"I didn't mean it literally," said John. "However, now that I think of what you said, it sure is our home and we are looking forward to being there." While they were saying this, they were packing, putting out the fire, and were ready to proceed down the river toward the lake. They were both eager to get home. The trip to the lake was very boring to them. It was the same thing they had seen for the last two days. Perhaps the fact they didn't see any trace that a human had been there helped their boredom. They stopped only for a few minutes to have the last of the soup and were soon on their way. It was about five when they arrived at the lake. The sight of the lake gave them some relief from their longing for home. They soon reached the raft. "Well the raft is still here," said Lora. "Too bad someone didn't steal it." Lora laughed harder at her own joke then John did although John thought it was pretty cute.

"What do you think?" asked John. "Do you want to spend the night here or do we keep going and get home whenever we get there?"

"Let's go for it." said Lora. "We don't have anything to eat anyway except a cup of coffee."

"I'm with you," said John. "Let's push the raft partially in the water so that we can pull it up stream. It will be easier if part is in the water. I think the slight flow of the water in the lake will have a tendency to drift us down stream." Lora didn't have to be told twice. She helped push it into the water and then taking one end of the rope helped pull it up stream. They were soon on the raft and John was paddling it across the lake. The flow of the water in the lake was unnoticeable. They reached the other side in about twenty minutes.

"Lets drag the raft as high away from the lake that we can get, suggested John. "You never know when we may need it again."

"How would we get it back to the river by the house?" asked Lora.

"I don't think we have to," said John. "However if we needed it there I could take it apart and carry it there. What I had in mind is that if we don't get rescued before winter sets in we may decide to go north as far as the river could take us. Sooner or later we have to run into someone."

"God forbid," said Lora. "We have no idea where it leads."

"I hope it will never come to that," said John. "You have to remember that we don't have heavy clothes for a winter stay. We wouldn't be able to go hunting."

"Well," said Lora. "We have the alternative to do a lot of heavy hunting so that we would stash away enough food for the winter."

"It's a definite possibility," said John. "It will have its problems also. For example, will the river freeze?"

"Let's go home," said Lora feeling overwhelmed with the problems. "We will worry about that later. God will take care of us." They tried to pull the raft as high on land as they could. It was hard and they were tired. They got it up to the first tree and gave up.

"Let's leave sufficient rope so that if the lake does rise it will just float up with it," said John. After tying it to the tree they put their backpacks on and started up the hill towards home. When they looked back they could see a part of the aircraft tail they lived in for a while. Lora felt a sense of excitement. But she also felt a strange feeling, a sense of a past horror and at the same time a sense of being near home. She couldn't figure out which she really felt most. Lora could see that John was feeling something also. It was almost seven when they past the shelter. Lora could see that John, like her, was feeling the excitement of almost being home. Their pace increased to a fast walk even though they were very tired. When they got to the house they dropped their backpacks on the kitchen floor and both jumped on the couch.

"It's so good to be home," said Lora. John didn't answer. After a few minutes Lora sat up and looked at John who looked more than just tired. Lora notice but couldn't put her finger on what it was. Because they were both tired she hesitated to ask him. But something was wrong and she had to ask. "John, are you all right?" she asked. "You look kind of sad. Aren't you happy to be back to the house? Is it that you are a little disappointed in the outcome of our trip?"

"I'm just very tired and I guess a little disappointed," said John.

"Why don't you go down to the river and get a couple of slices of deer meat," said Lora. "I'll stoke a fire in the stove so that I can cook us a dinner. I don't know about you but I'm starved."

"Ok," is all that John said. He then left for the river. As he checked the deer he saw that he had caught a fish on his fish line. It was still moving but barely. John decided he was too tired to clean a fish. They would have that tomorrow. He walked back to the house, gave the deer meat to Lora and went back to the couch. Lora cooked the dinner and included some canned vegetable and looked at John. To her surprise and shock she saw that John had tears in his eyes. He apparently was crying.

"Johnny sweetheart," she said nearly crying herself. "What is wrong? Is it something I said or did?"

"Oh no," said John. "You are the sweetest thing in the world. I love and respect you dearly."

"Then what is wrong?" said Lora sitting next to him on the couch. She hugged him and waited for an answer. John recovered a little before answering her.

"It is the word home that made me sad," said John. "We were both so happy to get back here and proclaim that this was our home that I couldn't help remembering my home in Ohio. I miss my children so much. I miss my daughter Sarah that I was supposed to spend time with in California. I miss the sweet love of Grace who is so gentle and intelligent. And I miss the little hotshot teenager that is so affectionate."

"I know my love," said Lora. "Are you very unhappy being here with me?"

"Oh no," said John getting excited. "You are the best thing that has happened to me. Can't I be happy being here with you and still miss my daughters?"

"I just want you to know that I have never been happier in my live," said Lora with tears in her eyes. "If we were in Ohio it would be perfect."

"Yes," said John, me too. I'm sorry for being such a crybaby. It was that word, home, that got to me."

"Nonsense," said Lora. "You're just a very sensitive guy. That's what I love about you. Now let's go eat dinner before it gets cold." After they ate they sat on the couch. Lora embraced him like he was her child.

"What are your plans for tomorrow?" asked Lora.

"I think in the morning I will dig in the garden and water the plants," answered John. After that I think I'll cut the grass. I haven't cut it in a while. How about you?"

"I think that I'm going to take a bath," said Lora. "Then I'll wash my clothes. If you take a bath, then I can wash your clothes at the same time."

"Sounds like a plan," said John. "You take your bath in the morning and I will take my bath in the afternoon. Then maybe the next day we can go around east of the area where the waterfall is, as we discussed before."

"Yes we can do that," said Lora. "We should have plenty of food and maybe we can get another deer as we did the last time we were there."

"For now let's go to bed, suggested John. "I'm sure you are as tired as I am.

The next day they did what they had planned. John dug around the plants and cut the grass while Lora took a bath and washed her clothes. She washed John's in the late afternoon after John took his bath. When John was digging in the garden he looked around to see Lora, but she got smart and took her bath on the other side of the dock behind the rock at the end of the garden. The next day they ate breakfast and set out around the rock by the river towards the waterfall. When they got to the wooded area they walked along the edge of the clearing but keeping behind the shrubs and trees out of sight. The land had a gradual rise so that at the end of the clearing near the mountain the rise to the waterfall level was more gradual. The hill was also covered with shrubs and high growth that looked like clover. They walked past the wooded area where John had obtained his wood for the raft. Suddenly John grabbed Lora and pulled her behind a shrub next to a tree.

"What's happening?" she asked in a whisper.

"Look there just behind that shrub half way up the hill," said John. "Do you see that animal eating the grass there? The sound it makes is like that of a goat. What is the sound a goat makes called? Is it braying?"

"No," said Lora. "Braying is the sound a donkey makes. I think the sound of a sheep or a goat is called bleating."

"Are you kidding?" asked John. "I never heard of bleating."

"I'm pretty sure," said Lora. "Bleating is the name of the sound both sheep and goats make."

"How did you get so smart," said John. "You are too smart for me."

"Since my husband was never home I had a lot of lonely hours which I filled with a lot of reading." said Lora. "Anyway, it not only sounds like a goat it also looks like a goat. Actually if you notice there is a younger one next to it with a young kid behind it."

"Let's slowly walk toward them," said John. "Keep your bow and arrow ready but don't shoot it unless it attacks us or tries to run away." They slowly moved closer to the goats. The goats made no move. They continued eating. John and Lora moved until they were across from them. The older goat looked up, noticed them but went back to eating.

"He saw us but it didn't bother him," said John. "They seem tame."

"I think you are right" said Lora. "Look at the older goat. Is that a collar I see around its neck?"

"It looks like a piece of rope tied around its neck," said John. After a short period of time he continued. "It all makes sense now. You found four boxes of cereal in the house didn't you?"

"Yes I did," said Lora. "I understand what you are thinking. Why would they have cereal in the house unless they had milk to go with it?"

"Smart girl," said John with admiration. "How could they get milk? They couldn't have it shipped in."

"They couldn't run down to the corner to get milk," said Lora. "They brought goats with them. They must be tamed like pets." They walked toward the goats as slowly as they could not to alarm them.

"Is that belt you are wearing needed to hold up your jeans?" asked John. "I need mine. My pants would fall if I took it off."

"No my jeans are very tight. I think they really belonged to the son." Without another word she removed the belt and handed it to John. John walked up to the younger goat and slowly tied the belt around its neck.

"Here," said John handing the end of the belt to her. He then grabbed the rope that was around the older goat's neck.

"Look," said Lora getting excited. "The younger goat has a kid and that means that the mother is still able to give milk."

"God is still with us," said John. "Let's slowly lead them back to the house. By the way, do you know how to milk a goat?"

"When I was a little girl," said Lora, "my uncle showed me how to milk a cow. He had a farm at Parkman Ohio. We visited him every once in a while, especially on a holiday. I guess milking a goat should be the same."

"You are a bundle of surprises," said John. "Is there anything you haven't done?"

"Lots of things," responded Lora. "I'm looking forward to doing a lot more."

"Do you remember when we first moved in the house that I told you that I saw a small ring in the shed and on the outside," said John deep in thought. "I also mentioned that there were two small boxes where one was lined inside with metal? They were attached with each other. I thing they are feeding troughs, one for hay and the other for water."

"Does that mean that the goat has to be kept in the shed?" asked Lora.

"Not at all," said John. "The trough is movable. Remember I told you that there was a ring on the outside of the shed. They probably moved them in at night." John slowly pulled on the rope of the older goat and it followed John without hesitation. The younger goat started to follow without Lora pulling on her belt. The young kid followed behind its apparent mother. It was old enough to eat some of the clover along the way. It was ready to be weaned from its mother. They were lucky to get them when they did. The mother looked like it still had milk. Soon they had them at the shed. John tied the younger to the ring outside of the shed. Concerned with the possibility that they were too late to get milk, Lora got a bucket and a bench she found inside the shed and started to milk the younger goat. After a little effort and practice she finally got some milk. She filled the bucket.

"What are we going to do with all that milk?" asked John.

"I had to get all the milk I could to make sure its body didn't shut down giving milk," said Lora. "We can use as much as we can and feed the rest to the fish."

"I understand," said John. He then tied the older goat to a stake he pounded in the ground. The old goat had headed for the garden.

"That could be a problem with these goats. We may have to take the older goat back to the other side of the rock where we found them."

"For now why don't you put a longer rope on it, tie it to the ring with the other goat," suggested Lora. "Let it eat the grass around the shed." He did that and they went inside to eat. The next day John took it back to the other side and let it go free. Later, when John was storing for the winter, he slaughtered the old goat and stored it for winter. They now had everything they needed to survive till winter. They had milk for breakfast, vegetables from the garden and two different kinds of meat for lunch and dinner. They would worry about what they needed for winter later in the fall. For now they were content.

CHAPTER NINE

The Worse of Days

John and Lora settled down to a daily routine. Every day was like the one before. John would dig in the garden, pick vegetables as they matured, and cut the grass when needed. Once in a while they would go hunting for rabbit and deer. They used the high grass and clover to feed the goat. The hours turned to days, the days into weeks, and the weeks into months. It was a late day in summer that John went outside and studied the sky.

"Johnny," yelled Lora out to him. "What are you up to?"

"I'm studying the sky," he answered. "I am looking at the position of the sun and the coolness of the air. I have lost track of the number of days we have been here. I'm guessing that it is about the end of August. We have to start thinking seriously about storing food for the winter. As we discussed before, we don't know if the river freezes or not. So we have to plan that the worse could happen. Therefore we have to consider all alternatives."

"What do you have in mind?" asked Lora.

"First we have to figure out how much food we will need," said John deep in thought. "At present a deer lasts us a little over two month. We have however been living high on the hog so to speak. If we limit eating meat to very small portions and only once a day, we should be able to stretch a deer to about three or four months. I believe winter would last from November through the middle of April. That means we will need food for five and a half months. To fill that need we need to have at least two deer in the water, at the beginning of November, besides as many rabbits and fish we can catch. That should be enough to get us through the winter."

"What about the possibility that the river freezes over," asked Lora.

"That's the other problem," said John. "I think we have to bring the deer indoors as soon as the river starts to freeze. I think I have to build something in the shed so that when it gets around freezing we can hang the deer in the shed. The shed should be like a refrigerator during the winter. I will cut the deer in half so that we will hang them by halves. If the meat freezes I can saw a piece as needed and defrost it in the house. We can also defrost ice or snow for water.

"Looks like you have everything planned out," said Lora with admiration. "I am really starting to think we can make it through the winter"

"Did you really have doubts?" said John, "oh you of little faith."

"I'm getting more faith every day," said Lora playing along. "But most of it is in God who sent you to me. Seriously, I really believing you can do anything with God's help."

"I think there is a complement in there somewhere," said John. "However we have a lot of work to do to prepare. It may seem like it is too early but better be early then late."

"What is our first move," asked Lora.

"We have to make sure the food we now have will last until winter," explained John. "We will do that by getting as much rabbit and fish as we can for the next two months. We have to hunt every day to get all the deer meat we need while also getting all the rabbits that cross our path. First I'm going to build a place in the shed to hang the deer for the winter."

"You really don't think that there is a chance that we could be rescued before then?" asked Lora sadly.

"There is always a chance," responded John trying to cheer her up a little. "The fall is the best chance. I had friends that flew to Canada every fall to hunt deer and catch fish from the river. So, there is a strong possibility that a plane may fly past here and see our sign and radio back to a rescue group. There is also a strong possibility that hunters may come here to this house or around this area."

"I've been thinking about that," said Lora. "Considering the goats we found I wonder if this place has been empty for more than a year. Would goats feel like pets longer than that? Also, would they leave all the tools in the shed and all the cans of food if they weren't expecting to come back?"

"You make a very good point," agreed John. "You have probably answered your own question. We could be rescued by the owners of this house. However, we should be prepared for the worse." John then proceeded to the shed. He fed the goat and checked for the wood that he would need. One of the shelves on the far right side had a very short section. He found the hammer and some nails and pulled a small three inch wide section of the flat three quarter inch thick shelf board. He cut two pieces from it about six inches long. He cut about three inches off the two by four that was now exposed. He drilled a one and a half inch hole in both the two by fours. He nailed the six inch boards to the top of the two by fours. That gave him an extension on the side of the two by fours so that he could nail them to the ceiling. He then went out around the rock to the woods to get a straight branch to pull through the holes in the two by fours to provide a pole to hang the deer from. He then returned to the house.

"Well," he said to Lora, "we are all ready to hang the deer for the winter. All we need now is the deer."

"We will get an early start in the morning," said Lora. "I don't think it will be a problem, do you?"

"We have gotten a lot of deer from the woods around us. I don't know if we can get two more from this area."

The next morning they got up early had a light breakfast and set out around where they had gotten the goats. They went as deep into the woods above the area the waterfalls were and hid near the upper river area. It was around noon when they saw a big deer with large six point antlers. They normally didn't see the male deer. What they usually got was a small doe. Between the two of them they shot the deer full of arrows. Even then they had to chase it half way through the woods. They had to go back to the shed to get the wheelbarrow. It was too heavy for them to carry it that far. They finally brought it home dressed it, cut it in half, and tied it to the dock and slid it into the river.

"That's one," said Lora, "one more to go."

"That's really more like one and a half," said John with a wide grin. "It probably will be enough to get us through the winter. However, it won't hurt to have another." The rest of the day went back to the normal routine. The next morning they started out the same as the day before. They spent all day and couldn't even see a deer. They did catch a rabbit which fed them that evening. The next day was the same. They didn't get a deer. When they returned that evening they did find that they had caught a large fish.

"Lorrie," said John the next morning. "I think that we are wasting time in these woods. I think we have to go back to the woods near the lake. We haven't hunted there for a long time. If there are any deer to be found it may be there."

"Isn't this the time of the year that they call deer season?" asked Lora.

"Yes," said John. "But they can't come out for the season if we have killed all the doe in this area." After a light breakfast they set out toward the woods by the lake. After two days without success, they went back to the house.. They went back again the next two days without any results.

"I think we have killed or scared all the deer within a ten mile radius," said Lora sadly. "What do we do now?"

"I think there is one place we have not visited as yet," said John deep in thought. "Remember the area between the shelter I built and the place the aircraft tail first ended?"

"Yes," said Lora. "That is around the big rocky area where you placed the big, help, sign."

"That is right," said John. "If you remember going east around that rocky area the ground goes down somewhat toward the east side of the lake. That is where the river goes east for a while before heading north."

"I remember that the area is very rocky with the rocks not being very high. The area is like large rocks were thrown around haphazard like."

"That's right," said John. "The area has many trees all around the rocks. I think that is a great place deer could hide and still go down to the river for water."

"Sounds reasonable," said Lora. "It is worth trying. Let's go there tomorrow morning."

"If we can find their path to the river we can hide behind a rock and wait for them."

"Sounds like a good plan," said Lora.

The next morning they got up early, ate a good breakfast, thinking that they probably would not get to eat until late, and set out for the new location. They walked past the old shelter, and headed around the mountain. They walked east for about a half mile across the clearing when the ground went gradually downhill toward the rocky area. At the bottom of the hill there was a large rock with several trees across from it.

"I think I saw some movement behind the rock," said John in a whisper. "Stay a few feet behind me. Have your bow ready if it tries to escape past me." John slowly moved to the rock. Slowly with his bow ready he worked his way around the rock. It happened so fast John didn't have the time to recover. A swing of a large bear's front paw knocked the bow out of his hand. The bear was standing on its hind legs. It was at least eight feet tall. As John turned to run the bear's powerful swing of its paw caught John on his left arm ripping a large cut on it. Before John could get away it swung at John catching him on the chest and lifting him in the air flung him against the rock. John fell to the ground. The bear moved in over him for the final kill. It happened so fast Lora was in shock. She quickly recovered and started to yell and growl at the bear. She had her bow and arrow ready to shoot. The bear suddenly stepped over John and headed toward Lora. He was so fast that Lora barely had time to shoot. As he was almost on top of her, his mouth wide open in a ferocious howl, she shot her arrow. It entered his mouth hard into its throat. It fell back on its hind legs trying to remove the arrow from its mouth with its two front paws. Lora took the occasion to shoot an arrow into its chest. As it fell backwards, she shot an arrow into its belly. The bear turn and dragged itself back passed John and disappeared behind the rock. Lora followed keep a wide distance from the rock. When she was able to see the other side of the rock she saw the bear lying by a hole in the hill dying. She also became aware of why the bear attacked John. She saw two small cubs walking around their mother. Being confident that the bear was dead she went back to John. His arm was bleeding very badly. She grabbed him under the arms and pulled him up the hill to the level area.

"Johnny," she called out. "Please be all right." But John was unconscious. Lora quickly found a small flat rock. She got John's Swiss knife from his pocket and using the small scissors she cut a strip of cloth from her blouse. Using the rock she paced it under his arm, being a nurse she knew exactly where to place it to stop the bleeding. She tied it tightly with the strip of cloth. She then cut another piece and wrapped the entire wound. She them checked him over for all his wounds. He had two big cuts down his chest. They were not as deep as the cut on his arm. He also has a cut on his forehead just above his eye. She could hardly see them now because of the tears in her eyes.

"Johnny," she called out. "Please wake up. I need you" She took what was left of his shirt, rolled it up and placed it under his head, hoping that he would soon wake and she could help him back to the house. When she lifted up his head she let out a scream. She found a large lump on the back of his head.. Now she was really worried. She remembered the story of the Hollywood star that died from a bump on the head. It was the same as John had worried about the bump on her head after the plane crash.

"Oh Johnny," she whispered into his ear. "Please don't leave me. I can't live without you. Please Johnny don't die." She then stopped to regain her composure. She had to think of a way to get him back to the house. She had concluded that if he was to wake it wouldn't be soon. She remembered that she had been out for four days. She couldn't leave him there on the ground for four days. She couldn't leave him there while she went back to the house for the wheelbarrow. Her thought went back to the shelter. Was the two wheel cart still there? It should be she thought. Because they had the wheelbarrow they didn't need it. She quickly ran up to the shelter. She opened the door and sure enough the unit was there.

"Thank you, Lord," she said. She grabbed the cart and hurried back to John. She laid the cart down on the ground. She pulled John by the arm pits and got the upper part of his body onto the cart. Then she got his feet on the end of the cart somehow. She really didn't believe she could get him on the cart, but there he was. She slowly pulled him up the hill to the shelter. From there it was an easier job getting him to the house. She pulled the cart handles first up the steps. She got him up one step at a time. She was glad there were only two steps. She moved the kitchen table and pulled him up to the couch. She removed the couch back pillows to make the couch area wider. She chose the couch rather than a bedroom because there was more light for her to work on John. The bedrooms were against the cliff and only had a small window on the sides. She removed his pants and shoes. Then she removed the wrapping from the arm to check the wound. It was very deep. Generally they wanted a wound that deep to heal from the bottom up. But Lora didn't have all the tools and nursery room available. She decided to try to suture the wound and hope that she cleaned it sufficiently to prevent infection. She got the medical kit, grabbed some cotton and soaked it with hydrogen peroxide. She cleaned the wound until her hands were tired. She then spread it inside and outside with antibiotic ointment. She boiled some water and after disinfecting a needle and some white tread she stitched the wound starting from the top. She then lined it with cotton and wrapped it with some gauze. She did the same thing with the cut on his forehead. The chest wounds weren't that bad so after cleaning them thoroughly she closed them with band-aids. She covered them with gauze and taped it down with tape. She then set the cushions that were in the back of the couch on the floor in front of the couch and kneeled down on them. She started to pray.

"Dear Lord," she started praying out loud. "I don't know what your plans are for us. I'm sure you didn't bring us here just to die. You know that without Johnny I will die. Lord you can read my heart. You know how much I love Johnny. Please don't take him away from me." She kept on praying until she was so tired she started to doze off. She didn't eat lunch. She wasn't hungry. As the day progressed she stayed on her knees. Dinner time she became thirsty and had a glass of water. For the evening she grabbed a blanket and tried to sleep on the cushions. Every once and a while she would rise and check John's temperature and his heart. They were fine. The night dragged on forever. But morning finally came. She check John again as she had done all night. There was no change. Also there was no evidence of any movements at all. She spent most of the morning praying on her knees in front of the couch sometimes holding John's hand. In the afternoon, she redressed his wounds to make sure no infections were present. At evening, she decided she had to eat something. She wasn't hungry but she opened one of the cans of soup, heated it and managed to eat it. The day dragged like the day before. It was the morning of the third day that Lora became extremely concerned. She had felt his head to see if he would wake and found that it was very warm. She checked his temperature and found that it was over 102 degrees. She checked his arm since that was the place she had worried about from the beginning. She unwrapped it and found that it was badly infected. There was only one thing to do and that was to pull out the stitches and clean it as she had done in the beginning. The surface had healed but the inside had not. First she had to sterilize a knife by heating it over a hot flame. Then she cut open the wound. Next she squeezed the wound so that all the infection was pressed out. She then cleaned it as she had done before. However now she had to redress it so that it would heal from the inside out. She took narrow strips of cotton and set them inside the wound. She then wrapped gauze around the wound. Now all that is left is to wait. It was just after noon when she found that his temperature had dropped to 101. She was somewhat relieved. However she was still concerned about the bump on his head. She felt his head. The swelling had gone down considerably. That was good news; however, she was concerned since after three days he had not awakened. It was a little past noon when she decided to warm up the soup she left the night before and eat. When she was done she checked John's temperature. It had come down. It now was 100. She decided to redress the other wounds. She had just finished when she heard a roaring noise. She suddenly apprehended that it was the sound of a plane. She grabbed a white table towel and went outside. The noise came from the direction of the old shelter. She ran as fast as her feet could carry her, waving the towel, down the path to the clearing where the help sign was. She got there just in time to see the tail of the plane disappear behind the mountain on the other side of the river. It was traveling north west. Lora thought it was probably the hunters that went to Canada every late summer. She fell to her knees and prayed. "Lord please don't desert us now. It is my prayer that the pilot of the plane saw our help sign and radioed it into the rescue peoples" She then, feeling very disappointed yet hopeful walked back to the house. John had not moved a muscle. The day slipped slowly. She fell asleep on the couch pillows in a state of depression. Although she had told herself that she trusted the Lord and was confident He would help. There was a part of her heart that was still hurting. The next morning came suddenly on Lora the first thing she did was check John's temperature. It had dropped to 99. It was about eight, as she was about to make some coffee, that she heard a noise. This noise she recognized immediately. It was the sound of a helicopter. She grabbed the towel and ran as fast as she could towards the area where the help sign was. It seemed like the path through the woods to the clearing grew longer. When she got there the helicopter was hovering over the help sign.

"In the clearing by the river," yelled Lora pointing in the direction of the house.

"What," said a fellow from the window facing her.

"In the clearing by the river," she repeated, There you will be able to land. Follow me." The helicopter had come lower so that the man heard her and gave her a thumb up sign. Lora ran down the path towards the house. she heard the helicopter over her head. It was faster and by the time Lora got there the helicopter had landed. She ran up to the man as he was stepping down.

"Inside," said Lora pointing to the house. "Johnny is very ill. You must help him." Two men jumped out of the helicopter and grabbing a stretcher went into the house and got John. They quickly brought him to the doctor who was aboard. Lora in the meantime although being in a daze, was able to collect herself enough to go into bedroom and collected all her belongings into her carry on suit case and also put all that she could find of John's belongings into what would fit into his attaché case and the rest she put into one of the plastic bags they had including the shoes and pants she had taken off when she brought him into the house. After bringing them to the helicopter she went back for the bags with the wallets and purses they had saved from the passengers they had buried. She was about to enter the helicopter when she remembered the poor goat. She ran to the shed and removing the rope around its neck released it. It went directly to the garden. Lora remembered that because of her total attention to John she had not feed the goat in three days. She then took a last look through the house and closing the door she climbed into the helicopter. The doctor was working on John.

"I hope this isn't a dream," she said as she got in. She became aware that the helicopter was not going to leave until given permission by the doctor.

"I see that you stitched him at first and then removed them when the wound became infected," said the doctor. "I see also that you redressed the wound so that it would heal from the bottom up. You did a good job. You saved his arm if not his life. Do you have medical training?"

"I'm a nurse at Marymount Hospital in Cleveland Ohio," answered Lora. "I tried, after cleaning very carefully, to see if I could heal it so that it would heal without leaving a big scar."

"It was worth a try," said the doctor. The helicopter was now in full flight headed south toward Denver. "By the way, I am Doctor Howard Brent."

"I'm Loretta Windston," sad Lora. "My friends all call me Lora."

"Who are you?" said a man who was seated next to the pilot. He was apparently the man in charge. "What is your relationship to the patient?" He continued. "How did he get hurt? Is that your summer cottage? I didn't see a boat or other means of travel. How did you get there?"

"Hold on," said Lora sternly, "One question at a time."

"I'm sorry," said the man. "Give me the information in your own time."

"As I said before my name is Loretta Windston," started Lora. "I'm from Cleveland Ohio. The man being treated by the doctor is Johnny Cane. He is a famous author. We are not related. The cottage as you call it is not ours. We came across it by accident. We don't know who owns it. John and I meet on a flight to Chicago. In Chicago we took the same flight to LA. The plane ran into a major storm. After the pilot tried to go around and over it, it was hit with lightning which knocked out all the electrical systems. After flying for about an hour it was hit again by lightning which started a fire in the wing. The plane crashed about a mile from where you found the help sign. We survived in the woods until we came across the house where you found us."

"You're not talking about flight 1114 to LA that disappeared back in April, are you?" asked the pilot excitingly.

"That is the one," responded Lora.

"We searched for months going back and forth between Chicago and LA. We went over 200 miles on either side of the flight line. We couldn't find any sign of the plane. You were about 500 miles from the flight path. How did you get so far from the flight path?"

"Where is the aircraft?" broke in the man in charge. "Before we saw you we flew around the area where you had the help sign. We saw no evidence of an aircraft."

"We did see a shining object just below the help sign," added the pilot.

"That is a piece of the wing," explained Lora. "John built a shelter for us that we lived in for a few week before we found the house."

"So what happened to the rest of the plane?" asked the man in charge again.

"We were in the last seats in the tail of the plane," said Lora. "When the plane hit the ground it spun around and severed the tail. The rest of the plane slide into the lake and after awhile it disappeared. Who are you?" asked Lora finally of the man who seemed in charge.

"I'm sorry," said the man. "I'm Alex Belfield. I'm the rescue squad manager. What we were told by the private plane pilot was so strange that I thought I would tag alone. Tell me, were there any other survivors?"

"There was a man but he was pierced through the chest with a splinter of the plane interior part. He only lived for a short while. I didn't see much. I was unconscious for four days John collected the wallets and purses and put them in bags. He then buried the bodies before I became conscious."

"How did you manage to survive for over four months?" asked Alex.

"John is a real sharp individual," said Lora with affection. "I believe he could do anything. He cut down the trees for the sign with a Swiss knife. He made a bow and arrow out of tree branches. He hunted deer and we were never out of food. He would dress the deer and tie it off the dock into the cold water to preserve it. He also knew of weeds that are not only good to eat but very tasty."

"Sounds like a real handy man," said the doctor.

"I wouldn't be alive without him," said Lora. "Doctor Brent. What do you think of John's chances? I see that you keep checking his temperature."

"I gave him a shot of antibiotic. I keep checking to see how well it works," answered the doctor."

"How is it working?" asked Lora.

"His chances are excellent," he answered. "His temperature is down to normal. I'm only concerned with the bump on his head. I gave him a sedative so he will be asleep for a while."

"You didn't answer the most important question," said Mr. Belfield. How did Mr. Cane get hurt?"

"I'm sorry," said Lora. "We were hunting for a deer when out from behind a rock came this bear. He attacked John before he could shoot it. I ended up shooting it. It took four arrows."

"I don't understand," said the pilot. "Most bears around here don't attack unless they are threatened."

"You're right," said Lora. "After chasing the bear around the rock I found it had two cubs. The bear attacked because it felt its cubs were in danger." From there on through the rest of the flight all were silent. All questions had been answered. Lora just sat quietly finding it hard to believe that they had been rescued. She sat wondering what was in store for them in the future.

CHAPTER TEN

Unexpected Events

About an hour and a half had passed since the helicopter took off after their rescue. The time, after the questioning period, passed quietly. To Lora it seemed like forever. Now she felt excited. She could see by looking out the window and seeing the outskirts of Denver that they were near.

"How soon are we going to land?" asked Lora.

"We will be landing in just a few minutes," said the pilot. "Denver Health has a helicopter landing pad. It is near the center of town. We will be landing momentarily."

"We probably will not be seeing you," said Alex Belfield. "I have a couple of questions that are bothering me. If that wasn't you property how did you get a goat? I suspect that it gave you milk. My other question is where did you get the seeds to plant a garden?"

"I was wondering why you hadn't asked about that," said Lora with a smirk on her face. "It isn't John's or my property. We lived in the shelter by the sign for several weeks. We saw the house, or cottage as you call it, when we went up on the mountain. The place you saw the goat was a shed that had a fantastic amount of tools. Among the many things like fishing equipment, bows and arrows, there was a variety of seeds. It was literally a hardware store. In the house we found a cupboard full of soup and vegetable cans. Whoever owns the house and shed had to plan on returning and being there for some time. We were hoping that the owners would show up and rescue us. As far as the goat is concerned," continued Lora, "We found it wondering on the mountain side. It had to be trained as a pet because we had no trouble bring it into the shed. Fortunately it had a baby kid and was still giving milk. We surmised that they had not left too long ago and would be back soon." As they were talking the helicopter circle the landing pad and was soon on the ground. Hospital personnel were there waiting for them. Two men were there with a gurney for Johnny and a nurse had a wheel chair for Lora. They were soon in the hospital. John was across the room from Lora. The nurse who said that her name was Krista settled Lora in her bed.

"Do I have to be in bed?" asked Lora. "I don't have any physical problem. I would like to see how John is doing"

"I'm sorry," said the nurse. The airline requested a full medical examination. It's also the law if they are to pay for your hospital stay, and I believe, if you want any retribution they will provide. Your doctor is Doctor Sam Brian. He is also Mr. Cane's doctor. Anyway, Mr. Cane is not in his room. Doctor Brian has him in the surgery room taking care of his wounds. As soon as he can turn the rest of the tests to the lab assistant, he will come and take care of you."

"What do I do in the mean time?" asked Lora. "I have waited too long for this to happen."

"I know," said the nurse. "I'm sure it will not be long. Do you want me to bring you a magazine or the newspaper?"

"Yes please," said Lora. "Bring me today's newspaper. I would like to read about my rescue." After reading the paper and realizing that the truth was slightly rewritten she set it down and started to imagine what life was going to be like from now on. Was John going to continue his trip to LA? Should she continue to see Flo her best friend? It was only about an hour later that Dr. Brian came into the room to Lora's ecstasy.

"How are you doing young lady," said Dr. Brian.

"I'm fine," said Lora. "What I'm more interested in is how John Cane is doing."

"We will see how fine you are after the simple tests I have arranged for you," said the Doctor. "The tests are required by the airline and the law. I did a simple surgery on Mr. Cane's arm. Who ever took care of him did a good job. Set his wound to heal from the bottom up saved his arm. His wound was almost fifty percent healed. That made it easier for me to close his wound.

"I did that back there in the woods after the bear attacked him, said Lora. "I'm a nurse you know."

"You did a great job," said the doctor. "His arm should heal just fine. It's the impact to his head that has me concerned. I am going to review his test results while you have your tests. When you come back I will discuss all the results with you."

"That sounds great," said Lora. "We got pretty close during our four month struggle for survival. I am very concerned about him." A hospital attendant came in with a gurney and took her to the hospital test area. She had CAT scan tests of her head, and her body where the side wound had been. She also had her arm, leg and head x-rayed. She got back just in time to eat lunch. When she had finished eating she went into John's room. He was there in bed looking better but still unconscious.

"I love you Johnny," she repeated several times. "I don't know if you can hear me as I did when I was unconscious back when we were in the piece of the aircraft tail. Please wake up. I don't know how to live without you." About an hour later the doctor walked into John's room.

"Well Miss Windston," said the doctor after walking in and looking at John. "You are perfectly well. We found everything is perfectly normal. Your leg and arm bones have healed perfectly aligned. I have informed the nurse that you are to be released. So please go down to the finance office and take care of that."

"That's great doctor," said Lora, "but what about Johnny?"

"The ex-rays and CAT scans show that there is no permanent damage. He is going to be fine."

"Why is he still unconscious?" asked Lora.

"The main reason," said the doctor with a smile on his face "is that I gave him a sedative. I want him to rest and be still while we give him back some energy through our feeding pick under his arm. He will wake up tomorrow morning. If he is mentally normal, we will consider releasing him"

Thank you very much doctor," said Lora feeling more confident. After the doctor left Lora get dressed and went down to the finance office and checked out. While she was down there a hospital employee stopped to talk with her.

"Miss Windston," she said, "Can you do me a big favor?"

"What could I possible do for you?" asked Lora being puzzled at the request.

"There have been several news men and news woman in the lobby all day yesterday and today. Would you mind talking to them?"

"Yes," said Lora, "why not? Perhaps I can get them to print the truth for once." Lora followed the young lady into the lobby. As soon as they saw them the news people surrounded them with every one asking questions at the same time.

Will you all be silent for a minute," asked the young lady. She will give you a statement and will not answer questions at this time. They all became silent. Lora gave them a short dissertation from the time the plane crashed to the time they ended up in the hospital. The information was sufficient for them and they all left quickly to write their articles.

"Thank you," said the young hospital employee. "They have been driving me crazy."

"Your welcome," said Lora. She then went up to John's room and ever though he was still unconscious, she talked to him until eight that evening. At a little after eight, the evening nurse came in to John's room.

"I'm sorry but visitor's hours end at eight," she told Lora.

"Can't I stay with him tonight?" asked Lora.

"I'm sorry but you can come back at eight tomorrow morning," said the nurse being somewhat unfriendly.

"I'm a patient here. I was in the room just across the hall," said Lora trying to wiggle an approval to stay the night.

"When you checked out," said the nurse, "you became a visitor."

"I know that in most hospitals visitors are allowed to stay with a very sick patient as long as they want. John has been unconscious for five days," said Lora. "That makes him very sick."

"They are allowed here if you are a relative," said the nurse," "a wife, brother, or sister. Are you a relative?"

"Well, we are in love and expect to be related soon," said Lora.

"Not good enough," said the nurse. "Please leave. I don't want to lose my job."

"I'm one of the two people that were rescued from the aircraft crash site," said Lora with a very sad look on her face. "Where would I go? I'm not from here."

"If you go out on Bannock street, turn right to the corner. That is 7th street. Turn left on 7th street about one block and you will come to North Speed road. Turn right and the Towne Place Hotel is right there on the right. It is a Marriott Hotel and is very nice." Lora kissed John and left the hospital. The hotel was just where the nurse had said. She went in and got a room. She noticed that not too far down the street was a shopping area. She went to her room took a shower and put on the set of clothes she had on her carryon case. She had washed them the day before they were rescued. Next she walked down the street and not far from the hotel she found a nice restaurant. Since she checked out in the afternoon she didn't get any hospital food, although she wasn't sure she wanted it. She was hungry so she stopped in. while there she asked the waitress about the shopping places near there. She was given directions and soon was back to the hotel with a new suit case and several changes of clothes. That night she had a hard time falling asleep. It was early morning when she finally fell asleep. She began thinking of the future with John. This caused her to become less anxious and more serine so that sleep came easier. Unfortunately, as tired as she was she didn't wake up until nine in the morning. And as you would expect the wakeup call didn't happen or she didn't hear it. She quickly dressed and prepared herself to be presentable to John if as the doctor predicted he would wake up in the morning. She then left as fast as she could for the hospital.

Earlier that morning John woke up wondering where he was. He realized he was in a hospital. Now he wondered how he got there. The last thing he remembered is being in the woods being attacked by a large bear.

"How did Lora get me here?" he asked himself out loud. He decided that it was some sort of a miracle. He them began thinking of ways it could have happened. He concluded that the only way to find out is to ask Lora. Suddenly he became aware that Lora was not around. Knowing her, he expected to see her bending over his bed. He then noticed a nurse call device by his bed. He pressed the button. It was only a few seconds later that a nurse showed up.

"Good morning Mr. Cane," she asked. "How are you this morning?"

"I feel a little weak and a lot hungry," he answered. "I am also worried about the woman, Lora Windston, who I believe had to come here with me. Is she alright?"

"She is fine," said the nurse. "She was in the room across the hall from you. The doctor gave her a complete examination and gave her a clean bill of health. She was released yesterday just after lunch."

"That is good news," said John, "but I was wondering why she isn't here. I expected her to be by my bed side this morning."

"She was by your bed side all day yesterday," informed the nurse. "She wouldn't even leave your side to eat lunch. However, As soon as she got released she became a visitor. Visitors have to leave at eight in the evening. She was forced to leave. From what the evening nurse said she didn't want to leave. She must care for you very much. I'm sure she will be here soon. Just as the nurse left a pretty lady walked into the room. It took John by surprise.

"Catherine," said John, with an astonishing sound to his voice. "What in the world, how did you get here?"

"Hi Johnny," she answered. "I'm so thrilled that you are alive. I thought I would never get a chance to tell you how sorry I am for the fight we had. It was the Lords doing that I'm here. I was in San Diego on business when I heard on the radio that you were found alive. I rerouted my flight home so that I have a couple of hours lay over here in Denver. I have to leave soon to complete the job. So I can't stay long. I have a flight that leaves in a couple of hours." She then moved up to John's bed. It was just then that Lora reached John's room. She was about to enter when she saw this beautiful woman bend over John, Lora waited for her to talk. She stayed just outside the doorway out of sight.

"Oh, Johnny," said Catherine, "Can you ever forgive me? You won't believe how I cried when I thought I could never tell you how much you mean to me, and how much I love you. Can you ever forgive me? I had no right to say what I did."

"There is nothing to forgive," said John. "I said a few things that I regret saying."

"Do you still love me?" she asked.

"Oh, Cathy," said John. "I will always love you. You have a permanent place in my heart. I never stopped loving you. You are all I have in this world besides my daughters." At hearing this Lora felt a severe pain in her belly. She remembered what John had said when Lora had asked him how many times he had felt butterflies in his stomach and lump in his throat. He told her twice. When asked who the second one was he said that it wasn't concluded yet and that the last chapter of that book was not finished yet. Lora was sure that this was that girl, and that she had found him and got him back. The tears filled Lora's eyes. She had lost him she concluded. She decided to run away. She thought she could never face going into the room and being introduced to the girl he was going to marry. She ran down the hospital hall crying with heavy tears.

"What is the matter, Miss Windston?" asked the nurse as she ran down the hall. "Are you alright?"

"I have to go," said Lora with a shaky voice. She ran down the hall out of sight.

Later that morning after Cathy left, the nurse brought John his lunch.

"How are you Mr. Cane?" she asked. "I have brought you your lunch. I know it isn't much but your stomach has to get working again after being without food for over four days. Apparently you didn't have a problem digesting this morning's breakfast. If you tolerate this meal I'll bring you more solid food for dinner."

"Have you heard from Lora?" asked John. "I am worried about her."

"I was going to ask you what happened between you two," said the nurse.

"What do you mean?" asked John. "I haven't seen her for the last five days."

"She didn't come in here this morning?" asked the nurse in surprise. "She was here and headed toward your room about ten this morning."

"She never came in here," said John. "What made you think we had a problem between us?"

'She never came in here?" asked the nurse with a bewildered look. "I saw her come from your room running crying hysterically. What was that all about?"

"She never came in here," reassured John. "What could have happened to make her cry?"

"I asked what the problem was and all she would say was that she had to leave," said the nurse. "I think she was holding something black in her hand. At first I thought it was a small black purse. However, it could have been a cell phone. Maybe she got a distressing phone call."

"She doesn't have any family that I know of," said John feeling worried. "The only close person that she has, that I know of, is Florence whom she was on the way to visit. In any case why wouldn't she come in and tell me her problem?" asked John not expecting an answer.

"Perhaps because at the time you had a visitor, remember?" said the nurse. "Perhaps she didn't want a stranger or anyone else to know of her problem."

"You may be right," answered John feeling depressed.

"I'm sure she will contact you soon and give you the details of her problem," said the nurse. "Now relax and eat your lunch. You don't want to upset your stomach." As she walked out of the room a young lady walked in.

"Sarah," yelled John with great joy at seeing her. "It's so great to see you. How did you get here?" Immediately he realized what a stupid question that was he quickly added, "When did you get in Denver?"

"I got here late last night," said Sarah as she hugged her father. "I got a room at the Marriott's Towne Place Hotel."

"What have you been doing all morning," asked John. "I thought you would have been here at eight. Did you over sleep?"

"I was here at eight," explained Sarah. "First I searched out your doctor. After talking to him and getting all the data on your health, I got him to agree to release you in my care. I then went to the front office and got your release. I had to sign a document that I would be responsible for your health after you were released. I also talked to your airline. I got two free plane fares to LA. They will pay for all your hospital bills including the ones for plastic surgery that I will take care of before I let you go home. I also negotiated a deal with them. It obviously needs your approval."

"What kind of a deal?" asked John.

"They wanted to settle for an amount less than they are negotiating for the deceased from the accident because you survived. I told them although you two were still alive you suffered over four months in a wild uninhabited bear infested woods. That you went through pain and hardship especially after being mauled by a bear. They finally agreed to give you to the same thing that they will settle with the families of the other deceased passengers. I think they are talking around five hundred thousand dollars. What do you think?"

I don't need any money," said John. "I'm so glad to be alive. If it wasn't for you and your new sisters I would have actually enjoyed it."

"Well," said Sarah, "don't tell anyone. For now get dressed we have a plane to catch this afternoon."

"Why the hurry?" asked John.

"Why would you want to stay here?" asked Sarah. John then told her about Lora.

"Don't get me wrong," continued John. "I loved your mother very much. But I never felt this way with any woman before. I didn't even know I could feel this way."

"You can tell me all the details about her on the way home," insisted Sarah. "We have to go if we are to catch our flight." John tried to sit up. He became very dizzy.

"Wow," said John. "I don't thing I can get up."

"You have been on your back for five days," said Sarah. "Just sit awhile and you will get better.

"The rest of the story is that she left here crying," added John to his story. "If she comes back here looking for me, and I'm not here she will worry. Her actions and her words the last four months assures me that she loves me as much as I love her."

"Why don't you leave a note with the nurse in case she does come back?" While they were talking Sarah was looking through the room closet. She found the brief case and the bag of clothes. Inside the brief case she found a pair of pants and a long sleeved shirt. In the bag she found his stockings and his shoes.

"Here, get dressed and I will take care of your girlfriend, said Sarah. What is her full name?"

"Her name is Loretta Windston." Sarah picked up the phone made a few calls and finally called the hotel.

"Hello," started Sarah. "My name is Doctor Sarah Cane. I'm trying to find information on a Loretta Windston. Is she registered there?"

"She was," answered the clerk. "But she checked out about noon in a panic. She was crying. She called a cab and left. I think she called the airline for Airline information. The reason I know this is that the airline called back with confirmation. I think she is headed for California."

"Thank you," said Sarah and hung up. She related the information to John. John had already put on his shirt and pants with great difficulty.

"Will you help me with my stockings and shoes," asked John.

"Sure," said Sarah, and with little difficulty she finished dressing him. "The clothes in the bag I think will fit in my Carryon Luggage. I left it at the hotel." Sarah got a piece of paper from the nurse and helping John write a note she gave it to the nurse

As they started to leave the room the phone rang. Sarah picked it up.

"Hello," Sarah said. "Amy, how are you guys?"

"We are all well," said Amy. "Is this Sarah?"

"Yes," answered Sarah. "I'm here with dad."

"Grace and I want to come and see dad. Tell us where you are."

"Sorry, we will not be here," said Sarah. "We were just leaving for LA. How did you guys find out about dad?"

"We heard it over the radio first and then on TV. "You can't imagine the joy we felt to hear that he was still alive."

"Here," said Sarah "Talk to dad." She then handed the phone to John.

"Amy sweetheart," said John. "I've missed you girls so much. I can't wait to see you both."

Daddy," said Amy with a tearful voice. "It's so good to hear your voice. We miss you so much we could just die. We wanted to come but Sarah said we shouldn't."

"Honey, she is right. You have to go to school and Grace has to work. I don't want her to lose her job. Speaking of Grace where is she?"

"She is right here Dad," said Amy. "She is too sensitive. She is crying too hard to speak."

"Tell her I love her," said John. "And I love you too. I promise to call you when I get to LA, and I promise to call you every day until I come home. Right now I have to go. We have a plane to catch. Give Grace a hug and tell her it's from me. Then have her hug you and that one is from me. Talk to you later. Goodbye." On their way out of the hospital John became curious.

"What are the plans from here on?" he asked. "When will I get to go home? I miss my house and the girls."

"The first thing we have to do is get your health up to par. You are very weak from loss of blood among other things. We also have to wait for your arm to heal completely before we can perform surgery."

"Surgery," asked John, "what surgery?"

"You can't go around with that ugly scar on your forehead and arm. I'm a plastic surgeon remember. We are going to get rid of those ugly scars."

"How long is all of that going to take?"

"I'm guessing that we need at least a week before we can do the surgery. If we can't do them all at the one time, we will have to wait at least a week before we can finish the rest of the scars."

"Do I really need this surgery?" asked John wanting to back out of the whole deal.

"You haven't looked in a mirror have you," asked Sarah. "Ask me after you look at the ugly scar above your right eye." John just smiled.

Several hours later they found themselves on a plane on their way to Los Angeles California. John settled in and started to tell Sarah about his time in the woods.

"Sarah you can't understand until it happens to you what real love is. Lora and I are like two parts of the same body. She is a very strong woman, yet I never met a gentler woman. She is the head nurse for a Cleveland Hospital. I think it is Marymount Hospital in Garfield Heights. She is very intelligent and always on top of things. She is very affectionate and loving. She is so beautiful that even after four months I couldn't stop looking at her. She is passionate and very romantic. She is a perfect cook and house keeper. I just can't say enough about her."

"Well," said Sarah, "after four months together and depending on each other it is understandable that you will have strong feelings for each other."

"No Sarah," replied John. "It wasn't like that. You see we met on the plane to Chicago. It was love at first sight. She happened to get a seat next to mine on the plane. I believe the Lord planned it that way. As soon as I looked up and saw her my stomach felt the proverbial butterflies. I got a lump in my throat. My mind became uncontrollable. I couldn't think straight. But even in that condition I could see that she was all flustered also. We started to talk after we got control of our brains. We couldn't hold back the way we felt. She said that she felt like she had known me all my life. I said that I felt the same. It was because I had seen her in my dreams all my life. When we found out that we were both going to LA we decided that we should sit together on the plane from Chicago to LA. Since she was on standby I thought that we could miss getting together on the plane. We exchanged names, addresses and phone numbers. She made it at the last minute but got the last seat in the tail. I had a great seat over the wings, but in order to sit with her I exchanged seat with a passenger who was glad to do it. It was all controlled by God, because Lora and I were the only survivors. The tail was the only part of the ship that didn't sink in the lake." John then went on to tell Sarah all the details of their experience up to the time he woke up in the hospital. "I have no idea how she got me from the woods where the bear attacked me to the hospital where I woke up this morning, five days later. The only thing I know is that with her nursing experience she saved my life." He continued until the pilot asked for them to fasten their belts and prepare for the landing in LA. An hour later John was sitting in Sarah's reclining chair. He was very tired.

"Dad, I want you to sit back and rest. It has been a very tiring trip. Even I am tired. I can imagine how tired you must be after your last few days, not mentioning the last four months."

"I want to call the girls," said John with the last bit of breath he had left.

"You get some rest for now," said Sarah. "It's too early anyway. I promise to call you after I make dinner. After we eat you can make all the calls you want."

“I don’t know if I can sleep,” said John. “I’m too worried about what happened to Lora.” Sarah ignored him and only a couple of minutes later John was fast asleep.

It was about five that evening when Sarah started to make dinner. She had been on the phone most of the time in-between. She woke John and gave him her phone.

“Dad, dinner will be ready in about a half hour. Now is a good time to make your calls.

“Thanks honey,” said John. “Before I call I would like a glass of water.” Sarah brought him the water and then went back to cooking dinner. John called Grace’s phone number. This time he got to talk with Grace and Amy both. After a half hour he promised to call every day and hung up. Then he called Bill and Sally his next door neighbors. They were just as elated to hear from him as the girls were. He told them a short version of his adventures during the last four months. After a while he promised to call them often and hung up. He decided to call the Denver hospital. He had the hospital and the room number in his wallet. He called and asked for Nurse Krista on the third floor. It was John’s luck that she was on duty and answered the phone. “Hi,” said John.” Is this Nurse Krista?”

“Speaking said the nurse.”

“This is John Cane. Do you remember me?”

Of course I remember you,” she answered. “How are you? What can I do for you?”

I was wondering if Loretta Windston returned to the hospital.”

“I haven’t seen her,” said the nurse.

“Did she call asking about me?” asked John.

No,” said the nurse, “not that I know of.”

“Thank so much,” said John and hung up. He then wandered into the kitchen.

“I’m sorry to be so long on the phone,” said John. “I had to call my neighbors. If you remember they are like family.”

"Of course I remember," said Sarah. "I also called Lora home phone," said John. "A recording told me that the phone had been disconnected."

"That is understandable," said Sarah. "She hasn't paid her bills in over four months. I hope she hasn't lost her home also. How about you?" asked Sarah. "I wonder if your phone is still connected."

"I'm so lucky," said John. "Most of my bills are automatically deducted from my checking account. However Bill and Sally have gotten my mail. Grace has picked them up, sorted through the junk mail and paid my bills. I asked her why she did that. I could have been dead and she would have lost the money. She said that she knew that God would not take me away from them. They still needed me badly. Isn't that sweet?"

"Yes that is," said Sarah. "They are gifts from God. We will thank God for them when we say grace for dinner. And incidentally, you are just in time for dinner." After dinner they sat drinking coffee and talked.

"While you were sleeping Dad, I got a call from my office," said Sarah. "They have been trying to get a hold of me. I purposely kept my cell phone off. It seems like Doctor Sam Wentry, one of the doctors in my office was in a car accident, and one of the other doctors is on vacation. I was planning on taking a month off and spend it with you, but I have to fill in for a couple of weeks. I will still take care of you. I have a surgery early in the morning and one in the afternoon. I will come home every day and bring you lunch and we will eat lunch together. I will come home early in the afternoon and will have plenty of time to cook dinner. I wasn't going to have you into surgery for at least a week anyway. I want your wounds to heal completely before we remove your scars."

"That's fine," said John. "By the way, when I went to the bathroom awhile ago, I looked into the mirror. I am now looking forward to the surgery. I hope you can at least remove completely the one on my forehead. I don't want the girls to see me this way."

"You will not know you even had a scar," said Sarah. "I promise. In the mean time do you want some magazines, Newspaper, to read?"

"Do you have any good book to read?" asked John.

"Dad, you being an author, I thought the last thing you would want is a book to read. Besides, I didn't want you to know that I had other books besides yours in the house," kidded Sarah.

"Strangely enough," said John, "I do a lot of reading of other authors. If I get tired of reading I can always watch a good movie on TV.

It was in the first day of the second week that Sarah came home and told John that the surgery time had been scheduled. It would be on Wednesday, the middle of the second week. John was nervous but still looking forward to it. Wednesday morning came quicker than John had hoped. Sarah drove John to the hospital at six in the morning. The surgery was scheduled for seven-thirty. They had some tests to perform to make sure John was physically ready for the surgery.

"Dad," said Sarah when everything was ready. "I'm having my boss, Doctor Walter Grafton, do the surgery. He is the best. He is the one that taught me everything I know. I find that it would be to.... What I'm trying to say is that I can't bring myself to operate on my own father."

"I understand sweetheart," said John. "I'm sure you would do a perfect job. Will you be assisting?"

"I'll be at your side every minute," promised Sarah. "By the way, I'm not sure that we will be able to do the job in one time. The scar on your arm is very large. We are scheduled to do your forehead first. Then we will do the arm. Whether we get to the chest scars depends on how much trouble we will have with the arm." They then gave him a shot and asked him to count backwards from one hundred. That was the last thing John remembered.

John woke up and found that he was in a bedroom and that the clock on the wall read two o'clock in the afternoon. He felt that he had just fallen asleep. He couldn't believe that six hours had passed. As he opened his eyes he turned his head and saw Sarah standing next to his bed.

"Hi Dad," she said. "How do you feel?"

"I feel like I was still in the hospital in Denver," he said and closing his eyes he nodded off. When he opened his eyes again Sarah was sitting on a chair next to the head of the bed.

"Hi Dad," she said. "You dosed off before. Are you wide awake now?"

"I think so," he said looking at his arm. It was all covered with gauze. "How did everything go?"

"I don't know if you are awake enough to remember this," said Sarah. "I will tell you that everything went perfectly. Not only that, but it ended that the arm wasn't as bad to fix as we original thought, so I'm glad to tell you that we got everything taken care of today."

"That is great news," said John. "When will we be going home?"

"Now what is your hurry?" said Sarah remembering that John didn't want to leave the Denver Hospital.

"I promised the girls that I would call them every day," said John.

"When we go home depends on you," said Sarah. "If you are a good boy and do everything the doctor tells you we might go home tonight. If not I could call them for you. I'm sure that they will be happy with the results."

"When will we really know the results," asked John.

"Why you of little faith," said Sarah. "Don't you believe or trust me?"

"Seeing is believing," said John with a giggle that told Sarah that he was pulling her leg.

"I see that you have your humor back," said Sarah with a smile. "Keep it up and we may get to go home tonight. One reason that it could happen is that I am taking the next two weeks off. That way I could take care of you.

It was a week later that they took out the stitches from all of John's wounds. The areas were still swollen and showed a narrow line where the scars had been. Sarah assured John that that would soon disappear.

"By the way Dad, I meet a guy that I have dated a couple of times. I know how you felt when you met Lora. I feel that way about Bob. I don't know how he feels, but by the way he has reacted since we met I think he has feelings for me to. He is out of town at this time. I don't know when he is coming back. I would really like you to meet him. I will call him before you leave and see if we can get together. I was hoping that he would call me for a date so I could make arrangement for you two to meet. Anyway, I will leave everything to the Lord."

"I do want to meet him," said John. "I'm so happy for you. I know he is wonderful. I trust your judgment."

"Anyway, you are well enough to travel around California," said Sarah. "So starting the day after tomorrow, tomorrow being Sunday, I'm going to show you California. "Before we do anything else I would like to show you some thing on my computer." She took John into her home office. "Look at my computer screen," she asked. John sat down on the chair and looked into the computer screen.

"Hi, Dad," said Grace. "You are looking so great."

"Hi, Dad," repeated Amy as she forced herself into the left of the screen.

"How in the world did you guys get on the TV?" asked John being very surprised and joyful at the same time.

"We are not on TV, Dad," said Grace. "Remember we bought you a computer for Christmas. We are in your house. We have been here at least twice a week keeping it clean. I hope you don't mind."

"Are you kidding," said John. "First of all I'm so thrilled at seeing you both. You can't imagine how much I missed you guys. "As for the house, I'll give it to you just to be able to hold you both again. You guys look so wonderful. I can't wait to get home."

"I'm glad to see you too," said Grace. "You look great in spite of all you have been through."

"Honey, I'm very grateful for all you guys have done. I thank God for you two every day. It has been so good to see you on the computer. We will not be able to do this again for awhile. Sarah is going to take me around California before I come home. However, I will try to call you whenever I can."

"That is fine Dad," said Grace and Amy in unison. Our desire to see you has been satisfied for the next few days. Have a good time." The picture of the girls faded from the screen. John's desire to see the girls was also satisfied for a couple of days. He did promise himself that he would call whenever he could.

Monday Sarah took her father all over LA including the old city. They had lunch there. They spent the rest of the day in Hollywood, what Sarah referred to as the movie capital of the world. They also drove through the city viewing the many beautiful homes of the stars. On Tuesday, Sara took John to Long Beach. There they toured the historic Queen Mary Liner. They toured the Queen Mary Museum, the Lower and Upper Decks, and the Cousteau's Living Sea. They had lunch in the ship cafeteria. When they got home, they ate dinner and sat discussing the next adventure. John called Grace and Amy and described what he had seen the last two days.

"How do you feel, Dad?" asked Sarah after he had finished his call. "Does all this traveling tire you? Do you want to go on?"

"It is great," said John. "It not only takes my mind off of missing Lora, but it gives me so much to tell the girls."

"Are you ready for a more exerting trip?" asked Sarah.

"Just lead the way," said John. "What do you have in mind?"

"I would like us to travel down to San Diego," said Sarah. There is so much to see down there."

"But isn't that a long way for a one day trip?" asked John.

"Oh," said Sarah. "It wouldn't be one day. It will probably be two or three days. We will stay in Mission Bay. Mission Bay is an amazing 4600-acre water wonderland. It would be a great place for an extended vacation. I've a friend there who will get us a couple of rooms at a great hotel." The next day, Wednesday, they took route 5 towards Long beach. On the way they stopped at San Juan Capistrano Mission. There they toured the Arcades, gardens and the imposing ruins of its ancient stone church. From there they traveled south to San Diego Mission. The pamphlet stated that it was built in 1769 and claimed that it heralded the birth of California. They then went into Mission Bay. They got a room there and after getting settled they had dinner at a luxurious restaurant. Thursday morning they ate breakfast and Sarah took her father to Sea World. They saw Shamu, the world-famous killer whale perform amazing feats. Afterwards they rode the sky-ride over the bay and viewed Sea world's magnificent landscape. On Friday, they went to the San Diego Zoo. Its size alone impressed John. It took all day for them to tour the complete zoo. John saw animals he didn't even know existed. To John it was a fascinating experience. When he wasn't thinking of Lora he enjoyed every minute of the tour. Saturday they went to Balboa Park. The fantastic architecture alone was worth the trip to John. From there they went to the N. Harbor Drive to the Maritime Museum. They spent all day there. The high light was their visit to the Star of India, the world's oldest merchant ship. Reading the information aboard ship, they learned that it was built in 1863 and that it was built of iron and by hand. That evening they dined in one of wharf's great seafood restaurants. That night they went to bed tired and full.

The next morning they went to a local church, ate lunch at one of Mission bay's finest restaurants and headed for home. They got home late that afternoon. They were both tired of eating out so Sarah made some sandwiches and soup from a can which satisfied both. After reading her messages from her cell phone which she had purposely left home and John made his call to the girls, she sat down with John

"Dad, what are your plans?" she asked. "Do you want to stay another week to rest from all the traveling we have done?"

"No, sweetheart," said John. "I've enjoyed these weeks with you so much, and I hate to go home but I think I have to go home.

Remember that I haven't been home for over six months. I don't know if I have a home."

"Of course you have a home," said Sarah. "I know that the girls have taken care of that."

"Why?" asked John. "Are you going to be home from work next week?"

"That's why I asked," she responded. "They want me in work tomorrow. I told them that was impossible. However I have to go in later tomorrow afternoon."

"Please call the airport," said John. "See if I can get on a plane to Cleveland." Sarah got on the computer and soon had reservations for John for 9:00 am the next day. The next day was full of tears. They hugged several times. Just as John was about to go into the security area, Sarah yelled out to him.

"Dad," she said. "I promise you I will find a way to come back to Ohio." It was about five that afternoon when the aircraft landed in Cleveland. Grace and Amy were there waiting for him. The tears between them were more than there was in the whole airport

"Dad," said Grace after they all settled down. "We have a fabulous dinner waiting for you at my house, if I must say so myself. You weren't fed on the airplane were you?"

"No sweetheart," said John still pretty emotional. "They fed me only lunch."

"Good," said Grace. "You should be pretty hungry by the time we get you home. Also the Stevens next door have invited us for dinner tomorrow."

"I miss you all so much," said John out of the blue. "I thought I would never see you all again."

"By the way Dad," added Grace proudly. "A couple of days ago we got the adoption papers. The adoption for both me and Amy were approved. All it needs is your signature. We also got your new will. That needs your signature also. And, as we told you over the phone, Amy and I have taken care of your house and property. The Stevens collected your mail and I sorted through it, threw away all the junk mail and paid your bills. I also deposited your royalty checks in your checking account. I hope that was all right with you."

"Are you kidding," said John with appreciation. "What would I have done without you?"

"You wouldn't have been as badly off as we would have been without you," said Grace with tears in her eyes which brought tears into John's eyes.

"Amen," said Amy. That sudden statement from Amy caused them all to break out in laughter. All the way home John's thought centered on how wonderful it was to be home again.

CHAPTER ELEVEN

The Long Road to Happiness

Lora was tired and not thinking straight when she reached John's hospital room and heard John declare his love for Catherine. She got a pain in her stomach that was unbearable. She questioned whether she had lost him. She remembered that John had told her that he had butterflies and a lump in his throat a second time and that it had not been resolved yet. He had said that he had not finished the last chapter of that book yet. She assumed that it was Catherine that he was talking about. Now she heard him say that he forgave her and that he will always love her. She decided not to go in. She didn't want to experience the humiliation of him telling her that he loved Catherine and was going to marry her. She couldn't hold back the tears and she ran down the hospital hall way passing the nurse who asked if she was alright. She answered her that she had to get out of there. She ran out of the hospital directly to the hotel, called the airline and found that she could get a fight to LA that afternoon. She packed her overnight bag, called her friend Florence, checked out of the hotel, called a cab and headed for the airport. The next thing she realized she was in the air headed for LA. As if she just came to from an unconscious condition she realized that she didn't really want to leave John.

"I love him." She said almost out loud. "I should have stayed and fought for him. What is wrong with me?" However, she was now in the air and there was no way to turn around. She kept accusing herself of stupidity. She tried very hard not to show her tears. She put her arms over her face and tried to appear as if she was sleeping. It seemed like forever but the plane finally landed in LA. Florence was there waiting for her. They hugged with great affection.

"I thought I would never see you again," said Florence with tears in her eyes. "I can't believe you're here. Pinch me. I think I must be dreaming."

"You're not dreaming," said Lora. "I almost wish you were."

"Now what does that mean?" said Florence being confused. "Aren't you glad to be here with me?"

"Oh Flo," said Lora with a repentant tone. "I'm sorry. I am so glad to be here with you. There is no place, actually, under the present conditions, I'd rather be. Let's get going to your house. I'll fill you in on the way." As they drove to Florence's house Lora explained about how she meet John. She explained how they were deeply in love for the four months in the woods. Then she explained how she did the most stupid thing by leaving when she did.

"I am so stupid," she finally declared. "I should have stayed and fought for him. I never loved anything or anybody as much as I love him. I should have fought for him."

"As soon as we get home we will call the hospital and you can make up some excuse as to why you had to leave in a hurry," said Florence. "Pretend like you never saw him with that other woman."

"Help me come up with an excuse," asked Lora."

"If by the time we get home we haven't come up with a good excuse," said Florence, "just tell him you will explain later."

"He is very intelligent, said Lora. It will be hard to put anything over him."

"Do you have any family members that you can say is close to death?" asked Florence.

"No one I can think of," said Lora sadly.

"That makes it really tough," said Florence.

"What would you do under similar conditions?" asked Lora.

"You know me," said Florence. "I like to tell the truth and take the consequences."

"I think that is the best," agreed Lora. "I don't want to start lying to him." When they got home the first thing Lora did was call the hospital. It was helpful that she had the hospital receipt which gave her the phone number. She asked for John's room number. There was no answer. She then asked for the third floor nurse's station.

"Hello, Nurses Station," said a woman's voice. What can I do for you?"

"Hi," said Lora, "I was looking for Nurse Krista. Is she available?"

"Just a minute I will get her," she answered. It was like five minutes or more before anyone answered.

"Hello," said the voice." This is Nurse Krista. What can I do for you?"

"Hi Krista," said Lora. "This is Loretta Windston. I've been trying to reach John Cane, but no one answers his room."

Hello Miss Windston," said Krista. "How are you? I was worried when you left here in such a hurry. Is everything all right?"

"Yes everything is all right," answered Lorna. "It was a false alarm. Is John all right?"

I'm so sorry," answered Nurse Krista. "Mr. Cane has been released in the care of his daughter."

"Do you know where they went?"

"No I don't" said Nurse Krista

"Did he ask about me?"

"No he didn't," stated the nurse, and then remembered the note. "Oh! wait a minute. He left a message. Let me get it. I have it. Do you want me to mail it to you?"

"Would you mind just reading it to me," asked Lora.

"No, I don't mind," said Nurse Krista as she started to read it. "Dear Lora. I hope everything is all right. The nurse told me you left in a tearful haste. You have my home number. Please call as soon as you can. Miss you terribly, Love Johnny."

"Thank you so much," said Lora. "Have a great day,"

"I think you must be mistaken," said Florence who had been listening on the extension. It sounds to me like he really cares for you."

"I'm sure he does," said Lora. "After all we spent four months trying to survive together. I care for you very much that doesn't mean I'm in love with you."

"Gosh," said Florence kiddingly. "I always thought you loved me."

"You know what I mean," said Lora. "Not in that way."

"Yes I know what you mean," said Florence with a smile on her face. "However I still think he loves you very much. He couldn't help it. You're too sweet, kind, loving, romantic, and gentle for him not to want you."

"I know you are trying to cheer me up. Maybe Catherine is that and more," said Lora.

"No, I have never been more serious. I've know you to long not to know that about you. Why don't you call his home? Maybe she took him to his home to recuperate."

"You may be right," said Lora feeling encouraged. I remember that after his wife died his daughter stayed with him at his home for over a month." Quickly she looked through her purse and found his phone number. She called but to her disappointment no one answered.

"Maybe they are not home at this time. Let's try every day," recommended Florence.

The days slipped by too quickly. Lora called John's home every day. There was never an answer. It was on Wednesday that she decided to try to contact John's daughter. However he didn't know her name. Since she wasn't married Lora looked in the phone book under Cane.

"There is a page of Canes," Lora said to Florence. "I can't call all of them."

Didn't you tell me that his daughter was a doctor?" asked Florence. "Why don't you look under Dr. Cane?"

"Why didn't I think of that?" said Lora feeling stupid.

"Because you are too frustrated," said Florence helping her check the phone book under Dr. Crane. There were three names with that title. However, there was only one listed under Plastic Surgeon. Lora dialed that number.

"Dr. Cane's office," said a young girl. "How may I help you?"

"I would like to talk with Dr. Cane please," said Lora hopefully.

"I'm sorry but Dr. Cane is currently out of town," responded the secretary. "Is there anything that I can help you with? There are other doctors who are filling in for her."

"No," said Lora. "I just need some information from her. Do you know when she is coming back?"

"She said that she needed two week, but knowing the life of the doctors she may come in sooner. Can I tell her who is calling?"

"I'm really a friend of her father," said Lora. My name is Loretta. I'm really looking for her father. I was told they were together."

"I'm sorry I can't help you. I'll relay the message," said the secretary and hug up. As things usually happen, Sarah never called in for any messages. Even if she had the secretary didn't write down the name and probably forgot it anyway. By the end of the week Florence got nervous.

"Lora," she asked. "How long do you plan on staying here in LA?"

"I don't think that I could stay longer than another week," Lora answered. "I haven't been home for almost five months now. I don't even know if I have a home. I haven't paid any bills in all that time. If I had my head on straight I wouldn't have come now. I should have gone home, straightened out everything and then come here later, probably next year."

"You probably wouldn't find me here," said Florence. "I haven't told you yet but there is a very possible change for me."

"What are you talking about," said Lora. "Come give me all the details."

"Well Dr. Willard has been asked to work on a very secret research project. He has asked me to go with him and be his assistant."

"That is wonderful," said Lora. "Sounds like a great opportunity. What does, go with him, mean? Where is the research going to take place?"

"That's the interesting part of the job," said Florence. "It will take place in Sweden."

"How long will you be gone?" asked Lora.

"The original contract is for five years, with a five year extension if the results are promising."

"I've been here a week already," said Lora. "Why haven't you said anything before?"

"It was only a possibility until now. That phone call I received this morning told me that it was approved."

"When do you leave?" asked Lora.

"We leave in three weeks," said Florence. "That's why I was so nervous this morning. I want to see all of California with you. Since we only have one week I want to start Monday. You can go home the next Monday and I can start packing and planning on what to do with my house. I don't want to rent it. I think I will have a real estate agency take care of it."

"Wow," said Lora. "That is over whelming."

Sunday after church Florence sat with Lora and planned the week. It was like a small miracle. Florence's plan was exactly like the plan that John and Sarah were to take two weeks later. They first visited Hollywood and the sights around LA. The next day they toured the Queen Mary liner. On Wednesday they drove to San Diego. They followed the same route John and Sarah would be taking later. They stayed in Mission Bay and they saw all the same sights that John and Sarah would see. On Sunday after church they headed for home.

The next day before Lora knew it, she had tearfully said goodbye to her best friend whom she may never see again and was on the plane on the way home. The plane, after a brief stop at Denver, reached the Cleveland airport about five that afternoon. Lora got a cab to her home. She had a difficult time opening her door. There was a stack of mail that had been pushed through the mail shoot in the door. She finally shoved her way in. She reached in and flipped the light switch to the on position, but there were no results. The electricity had been turned off. It was very hot and stuffy in the house. She took what she could carry out on the rear porch. It was a little cooler there. She quickly sorted through the mail and threw out all the junk mail. All she was left with were the unpaid bills, and the warning for nonpayment. The one she worried the most was the real-estate tax bill that was three months late. She checked her water and found that it was off also. She assumed that her gas was also off. She grabbed the bills and drove to the closest motel. To her surprise her credit card was still good. Probably, she thought, it was because she didn't use it for four months or more. What she owed was probably very small. She used it to get a room. She found some writing paper that the motel provided in the room and made a list of all the phone calls she would make early in the morning to turn on her utilities. She didn't sleep very much during the night. She had too much on her mind. Not only about the unpaid bills, but she missed Florence and of course Johnny. In the morning she called all the utilities. She explained all that had happened to her. They all agreed, having read the news paper about her. They all accepted her credit card. That taken care of, after trying one more time to get John on his home phone, she went to Marymount Hospital in search of her old job. She went directly to the main office.

"Hi Mr. Wesanick," said Lora. "How are you?"

"Well hello, there Loretta," he said. "I'm so glad to see you. From what I read in the paper you have been through a pretty rough time. How are you doing?" I imagine everything is up in the air."

"I'm managing," she answered. "Do I still have my old job?"

"Oh, Loretta," he answered. "That would be impossible at this time. We have promoted Jill Hosten to your old position. We don't have another head nurse position open at this time. But we are not turning our back on you. We will honor your many years of loyal employment. You will just have a job as a general nurse."

"Mr. Wesanick, said Lora in astonishment. "I have twenty years here and ten as the head nurse and surgical assistant to cardiologists. I cannot start from the bottom."

"I'm sorry but that is the only position I have at present. Leave me your name and phone number and I'll call you if an opening becomes available." Lora didn't even answer him. She just walked out in disgust. She went back to her house. Not all the utilities were on yet. She went back to the motel, grabbed the phone book and wrote down the name and address of all the hospitals that were within driving distance from her house and ones she felt she was willing to work for. Another requirement is that they performed heart surgery which was her greatest area of experience and expertise. That afternoon she visited University Hospital. She found that the answer was the same. They would start her from the bottom. She was told that they had many qualified and capable heart surgery assistants.

"I will not start from the bottom as a bed pan nurse," she told the employment agent. "I'm sorry" She then left the hospital completely disgusted. The next day she visited the Cleveland Clinic. They didn't even offer her a bed pan nurse position. In the following days she visited the Hillcrest Hospital, Saint Vincent Charity Medical Center, and Grace Hospital. They all had the same unacceptable story. On Sunday after Church, she sat down to decide what her next move was to be. She considered taking on the general nurse position offered by Marymount Hospital. After all she had many years there and eventually something would open up. After several minutes she decided she would not give up so easily. She remembered that John lived in Fairlawn, a suburb of Akron. Akron must have several Hospitals. The next day she drove down to Fairlawn. She got a room at the Fairlawn Hilton Hotel. It was on Market Street just a block away from John's house. After settling in her room she drove to John's house. It was around noon. She parked on the front turn around drive and rang the door bell. There was no answer. She walked around the back. The neighbor's drive was only about five feet from John's drive way. Lora walked the neighbor's back door and rang their door bell. No one was home there either. She then walked into John's back porch. She now was sure that John was not back from LA. Setting by the back door in the porch was John's old suitcase. The airline apparently had pulled the main body of the airship out of the lake and retrieved some suitcases. She wondered why they had not delivered hers. She returned to her hotel room and took out the local phone book which was provided by the hotel for the convenience of the patrons. She looked up Hospitals. She took the pad that was also provided and wrote the hospitals she planned on visiting the next few days. The list included Summa Health Systems. There were so many listed under Suma that she wasn't sure were to start. She noticed that one listed that it had a Cardiology Ward. She decided that would be the one she would visit. She also listed Barberton Citizens Hospital, Medina General Hospital, and Akron General Medical Center. Since Akron General was the closest by way of the freeway she decided to go there first. Early the next morning she headed down the freeway. It was easy to find since there were signs along the road showing the way. She parked across the street from the front entrance and was lead by the receptionist in the lobby to the employment office. She walked into the office and found that there was another woman sitting waiting to be interviewed. After a few minutes she spoke to Lora.

"Are you here for the x-ray operator job?" she asked.

"No, I'm not," responded Lora. "I'm here for a nursing position." They were about to introduce each other when a middle aged man walked into the room. At the same time a woman walked out of the office and addressed the man.

"Hello, Doctor Williams," she said "I'll be with you in a minute." She then turned to the other woman in the room.

"My name is Betty Whiting. I'm the employment administrator. I believe you are looking for a job in our patient testing facility. I called the manager of that operation and was told that the position has already been filled. No other position is available at this time. I'm sorry."

"She then turned to Lora. If you are looking for a nurse's position, I'm sorry there are no positions available."

"I have twenty years experience and over ten of those years as a cardiologist assistant. I can't believe that you have no need for my experience.

"I'm sorry," she repeated. Then she turned to Doctor Williams. "Won't you come into my office sir?"

"In a minute," said the doctor. "Miss, can I talk with you for a minute?" he asked Lorna.

"Yes of course," said Lora wondering what he wanted.

"Did you say that you had ten years experience as a surgical assistant to a cardiologist?"

"Yes even more surgical assistance if you include non heart surgeries," said Lora.

"I have a proposition for you if you are willing to gamble a few hours of you time," he said.

"I'll try anything as long as it's not illegal or immoral," answered Lora.

"You also have a sense of humor," he said. "I like that. Life is too dull without it. What I'm proposing is that you come to the hospital at about two and prepare to assist me in a heart valve surgery. Have you assisted in heart valve surgery?"

"I've assisted in a few," answered Lora. "Most of my experience has been in by-pass surgery, although I did a couple of heart transplants."

"Well come and assist me and if you do an acceptable job, I'll hire you as my personal assistant."

"What will I have to do as your personal assistant?" asked Lora.

"Let's get you qualified first. Then we will sit down and discuss your other duties. Just to answer a part of your question I have an office just down the street. When not in surgery you will assist me there.

"I'm game," said Lora feeling hopeful. "I don't understand why you don't use the hospital nurses?"

"I could, and I have. However, I would like to have someone with more experience, someone that I don't have to give directions to during surgery."

"I understand," said Lora. "I'll be back here at one o'clock."

"Good," said the doctor, "That will give me some time to show you around before the surgery." The doctor then walked into the office and Lora left. She went back to the hotel. On the way she stopped at

John's house. She went around the back to see if the suitcase was still there. It was. Lora went back to the hotel. She sat there and tried to remember every move that took place during that type of surgery. She understood what the doctor wanted when he said he wanted an assistant that he didn't have to give instructions during surgery. After reviewing what she could recall she promised herself that she would anticipate every move the doctor made and have the proper surgical tool ready to hand him. At noon she had lunch and was back at the hospital at one. The doctor took her through the Cardiology Ward and showed her where his patients were located, and where the next patient would be. They then went down to the surgery room, scrubbed down and prepared for the surgery. At two they started the surgery. Lora anticipated the doctor's every move. She also found herself holding the equipment that held the wound open. It was just passed four when they had finished. They washed up and removed their surgical clothing and headed down the hall.

"Well Doctor," said Lora how did I do?"

"Let's go down and have a cup of coffee and we will talk," said the doctor. Quietly they walked down to the cafeteria ordered coffee and sat at a table. "Well," started the doctor, "I hate to tell you this, because I don't want you to get a big head. But I have to say it anyway. You were fantastic. I thought that I had four hands. I want you in my employment."

"Can you give me a short description of what my duties will be?" asked Lora.

You will of course assist me in all my surgeries. When not in surgery you will first visit all my patients in the hospital early every morning. After that you will come to my office and assist me there. There you will perform all the tests that I have equipment for. Do you know how to perform tests using Ultra sound equipment?"

"Yes," said Lora. "I have some experience in the use and in the preliminary review of results."

"That is great," said the doctor. "The office is closed on Wednesday, Saturday and Sundays. The exceptions are that you will have to check on any patient that had surgery the day, before and of course in the case of an emergency. Otherwise, the hospital nurses will watch over them on those days. Because your time at work is so variable, that is, that some days you can go home early and some days you may have to work twelve hours, I am putting you on a salary. You will get a two week paid vacation." He then handed Lora a piece of paper. This is your starting salary. Everything is negotiable." Lora eyes opened wide. She tried not to show the emotion she felt. The salary was about three times what she was making at Marymount. "Do you have any questions?"

"No," said Lora. "I'm sure I will have some as we go along. Everything that you have said so far is acceptable."

"Good," said the Doctor. "Now, I want to know more about you. First I'm guessing that you are not married. So if this is true do you have a boyfriend?"

"I am single and I do have a boyfriend. He is currently in California having surgery to remove scar tissue that he got from being attacked by a large bear on our adventure in the woods."

"Yes I heard about the plane accident," said the doctor. "You and another fellow, your boyfriend I presume, were the only survivors."

"That is correct," said Lora. She had convinced herself that God would not have put them through all that they went through, if He didn't mean them to be together.

"What does he do?" asked the doctor.

"He is an author, Johnny Cane. I'm sure you have heard of him."

"Yes I have," he answered. "I just want to make sure you don't move after you get married."

"No we will not move," said Lora. "He can write anywhere. Besides, he has two daughters here. He would never leave them."

"Do you live around here?" asked the doctor. "I heard you say that your experience was with Marymount Hospital. That's too far to communicate from here."

"I do have a house in Garfield Heights. I plan on selling it and moving here. My boyfriend lives in Fairlawn."

"So what are your plans?" he asked

"I currently have a room at the Fairlawn Hilton Hotel. I will have to operate from there."

"I think you are going to need a few days to get settled in. I will start your salary as of today," said the Doctor. "Can you be here Friday morning for a ten o'clock bypass surgery? By the way if you are looking for a place to rent, my ex assistant is moving to Florida. Her husband has retired, and although she is too young to retire she resigned to be with him." He then wrote the address and handed it to Lora.

"Thank you," she said. "I'll check this out."

"So are we on the same page on everything?" asked the doctor. "Is the idea and the amount of a salary fine with you?"

"Everything is more than generous," said Lora. "I'll be there Friday." The doctor pulled out a document and started to write.

"By the way," said the doctor. "My name is Doctor Richard Williams. What is your full name?"

"My name is Loretta Windston. Everyone calls me Lora."

"Here sign this," asked the doctor. "It is our employment agreement. Read it carefully if you like." Lora read it quickly and finding it acceptable she signed it. "Ok then, see you Friday at about nine." Lora left as if she was on cloud nine. She went back to the hotel and called the Airline's Cleveland office.

"What has happened to my suitcase," she asked "Some people have received their suitcases. Why have I not received mine?"

"Some of the suitcases had name tags on them, said the clerk. "We could deliver them. The ones that had lost the tags are here and at Chicago. Some that we could determine came originally from Cleveland are here. If you can describe you suit case we can see if we can get it for you if it's not here." Having nothing else to do this late she drove down to the airport. Luckily, she found her suitcase. The tag had been partially destroyed. It did have the Cleveland number and Lora's first name. She had no problem retrieving it. She returned back to her house. The clothes, those that could be saved, were dirty. She placed then in the washer and went to bed. The next morning she called her friend Dolly in the real estate office. The result was that the agency would get an estimate of the value of her property and get back to her. Together then they would determine the sale price. Lora then returned to her room in the Fairlawn Hotel where most of her good clothes were. She took a shower and went to the address the doctor had given her. No one was there but there was a sign giving the name, address, and phone number of the agency. Since it was located just around the corner she went directly to the Real Estate office.

"My name is Rose," said the girl at the desk in the entrance way. What can I help you with?"

"I am interested in the apartment that is for rent on Miller Road." said Lora. "What is the rent?"

"I'm sorry, said Rose. "That has just been sold. I have not had the chance to change the sign. Is there anything else I can show you?"

"I'm interested in a small apartment where I may only stay for less than a year," said Lora trying to be honest. "My boyfriend and I plan on getting married. We have not set a date yet so it may be a few months. I have a lot of furniture at a house I'm trying to sell in Garfield Heights."

"That is quite a requirement," said Rose. "I'm glad you are honest. Most renters want at least a year contract. Wait," she said thinking of a possibility that just entered her mind. "I may have a proposition for you. Are you a gambler?"

"Try me," said Lora looking for anything to move into as soon as possible.

"I have a small ranch house right here in Fairlawn that is for sale. It's a two bedroom house with a living room and a kitchen. The owners, an older couple, moved to Arizona and have been trying to sell the property. However, to pay the tax they are willing to rent it. There are two problems. One is that there is a lot of work to be done to get it back into selling shape. The other is that while you are in there you must allow potential buyers in to see the house."

"Sounds interesting," said Lora. "What are the details? What is the rent?"

"You will patch the holes in the plaster and paint all the rooms. The couple that rented it last had an unruly son who with his tricycle put holes in the walls. They stayed two years and never did any cleaning. We will supply all the paint and equipment. You will provide the labor. You pay for the painters if you hire it out. The monthly rent will be two hundred fifty dollars a month.

"Let me think about that," said Lora. "In the mean time see if you could come up with another possibility." Lora then left deep in thought. First she had to move fast in order to go to work as needed. Secondly she figured she had nothing to do at night until John comes home. Maybe fixing the house was a good idea. The rent was more than reasonable. A house usually rents for between five hundred and a thousand a month. Of course she will have to look at the house first. What finally made up her mind was when Dolly called.

Hi Dolly," said Lora. "What did you find out?"

"The house was evaluated at one hundred seventy thousand dollars," said Dolly. "However, the homes in the neighborhood have sold for one hundred sixty thousand. So what do you think?"

"What are the cost going to be after the sale?" asked Lora.

"I think they should be somewhere just below twenty thousand."

"Do you think we can get one sixty?"

"I think so. Incidentally, for something for you to think about, I have a young couple who are looking for a house around one fifty. If you sold it to them you would clear somewhere above one thirty. I will also be willing to cut my real estate fee, if you decide to sell to them."

"I don't even what to think about it," said Lora. "Go ahead and see if they like my house. I'm not going to wait for ten thousand more. A quick sale is worth it."

"All right then," said Dolly. "I will let you know as soon as I can talk with them." Lora was happy with the idea of possibly getting this of out of the way. Now she had to worry about taking care of her furniture. She called Rose in the Real Estate Office

"Rose," said Lora, "When can you show me the house we were talking about?"

"What are you doing now?" asked Rose. "I don't have an appointment for about two hours. How soon can you get here?"

"I'll be there in two minutes," said Lora. Soon the two of them were at the house. Lora looked over the work that had to be done. She decided that it was within her capabilities. The house was nicer than she had expected. Rose had forgotten that the house also had a dining room and a lovely rear screened enclosed porch. Lora quickly determined why it was hard to sell when they checked the outside. The far end of the lot had a high hedge. However from the rear porch, one could see above the hedge. The area behind the hedges was the Rose Hill Burial Park, a cemetery. It brought a smile on Lora's face.

"I'll take the deal," said Lora. "When can I move in?"

"You can move in as soon as you sign some papers and pay a first month's rent." After that was done, Lora returned to her house in Garfield Heights. She called a mover. She found that they could come early Thursday morning. Lora then went into the house and put everything she didn't need in the garage. She then packed what she could of her personal things in boxes and when she ran out of boxes she stuffed the back seat and trunk of her car. Thursday morning the movers loaded everything Lora told them to, and they were ready to travel. She left the old refrigerator and some old living room chairs. By noon they had everything unloaded. Lora paid the bill and went inside to settle things. After some lunch at a fast food cafe, she went to Loews for some paints and painting equipment. She also got some Plaster Patch. The clerk told her that for small jobs, Plaster Patch was best because it was already mixed and was like putty. She also got a putty knife to spread it with. That night Lora patched all the holes in the walls. She moved the bed and furniture to the center of the room covering it all with an old blanket she was going to throw away making it ready for painting. At two that afternoon she started to pain the bedroom. By that evening she had finished it, went for dinner, and came back to give it a second coat. That done she went to the hotel for the night. The next morning she was at Akron General for the surgery with Doctor Williams. She informed him where she was in her moving he told her to go home after the surgery and he would take care of visiting the patient the next morning. That afternoon she painted the other bedroom and finished it by evening. On Saturday and Sunday after church she finished the other two rooms and the kitchen. On Monday morning before the scheduled surgery she went to Rose at the Real Estate office and handed her a spare set of keys to the house. Lora explained that she had the locks changed. After surgery the next day she checked out of the hotel and moved in her new home. A couple of week went by under extremely busy days at the hospital. Doctor Williams had proponed surgeries that could be delayed because of not having an acceptable nurse and because of Lora's unavailability, due to her moving. Lora house in Garfield Heights was finally sold. The schedule and Lora were now more relaxed. Finding time she went to John's house to see if he was home yet. In the back yard, Lora noticed that a neighbor was out watering her flowers. He walked over to her.

"Hi," she said. Can you tell me if Mr. Cane has come home yet?"

"No," said Sally. "Are you another news lady? We have been harassed enough for the news people."

"No," said Lora. "I am a close friend. Actually I'm a nurse."

"John is still in California," said Sally. "He just got out of surgery. He had scar tissue removed."

"Do you have any idea when he will come home?"

"We have no idea," said Sally. He is with his daughter. He will probably spend some time with her." As Lora started to walk away Sally asked, "Can I tell him who you are when he comes home?"

"Just tell him that a friend called." Lora didn't want John to know that she was looking for him. She didn't want him to think up an excuse if he needed one. She went back to her normal every day routine. She loved her new job. She fit in like she had been born to it.

John was very happy to be home with Grace and Amy. However he missed Sarah and most of all Lora. The second night home they all were invited to Bill and Sally's home for dinner. All through dinner he thought of Lora. What happened to her? The next day he knew he had to find Lora. Early in the morning he left to find Lora's house in Garfield Heights. He had her address from the card she had given him in the plane to Chicago. It took him about a half hour to find her house. He became concerned when he saw the sold sign on her front yard. He pulled in the drive and walked up to the front door. He rang the door bell and after getting no response he knock on the door. He still got no response. He moved to the right where he could look into the living room window. He became depressed when he realized that the house was completely empty of any furniture. He got the Real Estate office phone and called it when he got home. Unfortunately Lora's girlfriend was off that day and a man answered the phone.

"May I help you?" said a male voice.

"Yes the house on York Road in Garfield Heights has been sold. Can you tell me where the previous owner moved to?"

"The previous owner?" asked the man.

"Yes please," said John

"Just a minute, I'll look at our records," he said. A few minutes later he returned. "I'm sorry; our records do not have that information." John hung up completely dejected. He then decided that God will have to bring them together. He was sure he would in his own time. Believing this the next day John went to his jeweler. He bought a beautiful ring with a large diamond. He also bought a wedding band that attached to the engagement ring. He wanted to be prepared when God would bring Lora to him.

During the day everyone was either in school or working. To keep busy he returned to the Soup Kitchen. He spent a week there helping where ever help was needed. The next week on Wednesday he decided not to go. He checked his freezer for food that he had to throw away and what he could keep. That evening he called Grace.

"Hi Grace," he started. "How are you guys?"

"We are fine, Dad," she responded. "What's up?"

"What are you, Amy, and Paul doing this Friday?"

"We don't have any plans except that Paul is coming over Friday. He is out of town for a couple of days but will come home Thursday night. What do you have in mind? We would love to spend time with you."

"I was cleaning out my freezer," said John. "I hadn't even opened it for over five months now. I had to throw out a lot of stuff. Fortunately Annie liked to date everything in the freezer. I continued that practice. Any way I found a large seventeen pound ham that was dated about six months ago. I originally thought I could make it for Thanksgiving. Then if you remember, Bill and Sally had insisted that for old time sake we spend Thanksgiving with them. So I decided to invite them this Friday and we will have our own pre-thanksgiving dinner."

"Dad, that sounds great. We will love that. What do you want me to bring?"

"I would like you to bring Amy and Paul," said John.

"Dad, you know what I mean," said Grace with laughter.

"Honey, said John. "I think I'll make some of that microwave frozen vegetable and a salad. I think that will be sufficient."

"Then I'll bring some potatoes and some soup," said Grace with determination in her voice.

"That will be fine, honey," said John.

"Dad, what have you been up to?" asked Grace. "I've called you a few times in the evening and you have never been home."

"Honey," answered John. "I've spent the last week or so at the Soup Kitchen. I've been worried about Lora. But now I decided that it was up to God to bring us back together. I will not be going as often now. I've started to write again. I want to write about Lora and my romantic adventure."

"That is so great," said Grace. "I'm looking forward to reading it."

"All right Honey," concluded John "See you on Friday"

"Dad it will be the longest two days I've ever had. Love you, good night" John spent the next two days reviewing what he was going to write. The first problem was where he was going to start. He wasn't sure if he should write it as just another novel or should he write his memoirs. He decided to start with the airplane flight to Chicago. Then if he decided to write it as his memoirs he would just add to it. He would discuss it with his girls and Paul, Grace's boyfriend. Friday came faster for him than it did for the girls. John had taken the ham out of the freezer and put it into the refrigerator to thaw on Monday. About Friday noon he took it out of the refrigerator and prepared it for cooking. From the weight and the instructions on the label he figured it would take about four hours to cook. He placed a thermometer in the center of the ham. Annie and John cooked ham once in a while. Because they liked Tavern Ham which came in larger package, they always had more than they could eat. They would cut the ham into quarters and freeze three of the pieces. They would eat the other quarter for the next couple of days. Months later they would take a piece out of the freezer and after it thawed they would slice it and have it on sandwiches or with eggs in the morning as ham and eggs. He had planned on doing the same thing with this ham. He felt that the six would not eat more than a quarter of the ham. If necessary he would cut another quarter as needed. He would not freeze any until that night after all had left. At two he put the ham in the oven. It was four when the rear door bell rang. It was Grace, Paul and Amy.

"Hey you guys," said John. "You are two hours early. Not that I'm not glad that you are here. I just didn't expect you. Come on in. I have the ham in the oven so I'm free for awhile." John hugged all three. They came into the family room but didn't sit down.

"We came early because we wanted to include you in our celebration and this joyful occasion." As she said that, she stuck out her hand. The ring was clearly visible.

"Wow," said John. "That ring is so beautiful and brilliant that it almost blinds me."

"Paul asked me to marry him," said Grace with a joyful smile. I just had to come and tell you about it."

"That is the best news I have ever hear," said John as he hugged them both. Grace saw tears in his eyes.

"Daddy, I'm so happy that you approve," said Grace.

"I approved of him when I met him before my ill fated trip. I think you two were made for each other." Just as he had said that the front door bell rang.

"I wonder who that could be," said John.

"You invited Bill and Sally didn't you?" asked Grace. "Could that be them?"

"I don't think so," said John. "They would come through the back not the front." John went into the foyer and answered the front door. When he saw who it was, his eyes lit up. "Lorrie" he yelled out. "It's so good to see you." He then grabbed her and gave her a loving hug. She didn't return his affection. She stood erect like a cold lamp pole. John noticed her cold reception.

"Lorrie honey," he said with a frown on his face. "What is wrong?" he asked.

"Do you love Catherine with all your heart?" she asked.

"What are you talking about?" asked John now being very puzzled. "What do you have to do with Catherine? What is this all about?"

"Don't dodge the question," said Lora being very serious.

"Of course I love Catherine. How do you know about her? What are you babbling about?"

"When I came to the hospital the next day I came to your room and saw you and this beautiful girl kissing each other and heard you both declare your love for each other. You called her Catherine."

"Why didn't you stop in and give me a chance to explain everything to you?" said John now beginning to understand her problem.

"Don't beat around the bush," said Lora getting angry. "Are you going to marry Catherine?"

"What makes you think that I want to marry her?"

"Just answer the question," she insisted. "Are you going to marry Catherine?"

"No I'm not going to marry Catherine," said John now in full understanding. "I don't even know if it is even legal in this state."

"Why wouldn't it be legal," asked Lora now being confused. "Is she still married or something?"

"No she is still single or rather widowed," answered John. "It's just that I don't think it is acceptable for a man to marry his own sister."

"Oh, dear Lord," said Lora in deep shock. "Catherine is your sister?"

"We have the same mother and father I think that makes us brother and sister."

"Go ahead and rub it in," said Lora. "I certainly deserve it."

"What made you jump to the idea that she would be my girlfriend," asked John as he pulled her into the family room where Grace, Paul and Amy were sitting and hearing every word.

I remember when we were on the plane from Chicago to LA that you mentioned that you experienced butterflies in your stomach and a lump in your throat twice in your life time. The first was Cora in college and the second you said was still pending. You said that the last chapter of that book was not finished. I thought that was Catherine, so then who is that woman that gave you butterflies in your stomach and a lump in your throat?"

"Lora," said John. "Do you know that you can be such an idiot?"

"Why am I an idiot?" asked Lora.

"You are an idiot because you should have known that that other woman who gave me butterflies and a lump in my throat is you. At the time I didn't know how our relationship would turn out,"

"Dear Lord," said Lora and sat down on a near chair. "I am such an idiot. Why didn't I think of that? I'm such an idiot" she repeated. "Oh Johnny, can you ever forgive me?"

"I don't know," said John. "Jealousy has destroyed many relationships, even ended many marriages."

"What will it take to make this up to you?" asked Lora. "I promise that I will never be jealous again. I will trust you completely. I'm not only an idiot but I'm pretty stupid. I admit it."

"You're not stupid and not an idiot most of the time," said John. I don't know when I will be able to forget or forgive you, but the only thing I can tell you for sure is that I will love you with all my heart forever and I want to spend the rest of my life with you. I have been so miserable without you." At that Lora got up and hugged John and gave him a passionate kiss. The kiss was the most passionate kiss he had ever received. It lasted longer than it should have.

"I have been going out of my mind missing you," said Lora. "I didn't think I could live without you."

"I'm sorry guys," said John turning to the kids sitting watching

"That's all right Dad," said Grace. "It was entertaining. It was like watching a soap opera." Everyone laughed. John and Lora did also but with red faces.

"Lora," said John. "I want you to meet my daughter Amy, my daughter Grace, and Paul, Grace's fiancé, Guy's, as you have surmised this Loretta Windston." They all hugged and exchanged greetings.

"Girls," said Lora, "I feel like I've know you all my life. John never stopped talking about you all." Just then the door bell rang again.

"Now who could that be at the front door?" asked John puzzled. "Everyone except the Stevens are here." John went to the front door and opened it. At the door were a young lady and a young man.

"Sarah," yelled John. "What a surprise to see you. I just left you in LA." John then hugged her and kissed her on the cheek.

"Well there are two more surprises for you, Dad," said Sarah then hearing a lot of commotion in the family room she asked. "I hear a lot of commotion, do you have company?"

"Just the girls," said John wanting to hear of the surprise. "First, I want you to meet Robert Bensen," said Sarah.

"I heard about you when I was in LA. I guess you're her boyfriend, I wanted to meet you but you were out of town" John then hugged him. "Now what are the surprises you have for me? It's too early for Christmas presents."

First is this," said Sarah holding out her hand. On her finger was a large beautiful diamond ring. "Bob asked me to marry him."

"My Lord," said John, hugging them both "Two in one night is fantastic."

"Two in one night?" asked Sarah. "What does that mean?"

"Come inside and you will see," said John.

"I can hardly wait," said Sarah." They walked inside and after introducing Paul, they showed each other their rings. "Also," said John turning to Lora, "this is Lora that you have heard so much about while I was in LA." Sarah hugged Lora. I hear so much about you and how much he loves you that I almost feel like calling you, Mom."

I would love nothing better than to make that official," said Lora hinting to John.

"By the way Sarah," said John. "You said that you had two surprises. What is the second?"

"I almost forgot with all the good news I'm hearing. The reason you didn't get to meet Bob is that Bob was up here looking for a place for us to move our practice. We found one and we have purchased it. We will be moving here in a few days. We bought a building near Akron General Hospital on Cedar road just east of Wabash."

"That is fantastic," said Lora. "The office where I work is in the same place, maybe the same building."

"I don't think it's the same building," said Sarah, "because our building is small and only has two doctor's offices. But next door is a large medical office building."

"That is where I work," said Lora excitingly.

"That is great, said Sarah. "We will go to lunch together some times.

"Wonderful," said John. "It makes us one big family. Where are you and Bob staying?"

"We plan, with your help to find a small house we could rent or possible buy. For now, we checked in to the Hilton on Market Street."

"That is such wonderful news," said John. "Yesterday I was alone and now I'm part of one big loving family."

"Johnny," said Lora changing the subject. "You said that you wanted to spend the rest of your life with me. Was that a proposal?"

"That was a pre-proposal," said John.

"What does that mean?" asked Lora.

"It means that a proposal is not valid without a ring," said John.

"I don't need a ring," said Lora. "All I need is a wedding band."

"Just wait a minute," said John. "I have something important to do. I'll be right back." John went upstairs and came back a few minutes later. "I didn't expect to see you this soon. So I wasn't prepared." John then pulled Lora to a chair and made her sit down. Lora wasn't dumb. She figured out what was coming. Tears ran down her face. John got on his knees.

"Lora, "he began. "You are the only one who has given me butterflies in my stomach and a lump in my throat since my college days, and they seem to get more aggressive. Will you marry me?"

"Yes," she said barely getting it out of her mouth because of her crying. She then got up and threw herself into his arms.

"I guess there is going to be three wedding soon," said Grace. "Are we all going to get married together?"

"No way," said Sarah. "I want dad to walk me down the aisle. Don't you want dad to walk you down the aisle?"

"You are so right," said Grace. "What was I thinking of?"

"Not only that," said Sarah, "I want you Grace, to be my Maid-of-Honor."

"I don't have a best friend here that I could count on," said Bob. "I would like Paul to be my Best Man, if he will agree."

"I would be honored," said Paul. "After all you are going to be my brother-in-law.

"Now the question is who is going to get married first," said Sarah. "Grace do you know who want to stand up for you two?"

"Yes," said Grace. "Paul has a brother that he wants to be his best man, and I want Amy to be my Maid-of-Honor."

"Great," said Sarah. "You can get married right after me, since you don't need anyone except Dad."

"No," said Grace."I want you to come to my wedding as I'm sure you want me to come to your wedding."

"Girls listen to me," said John. "While you girls were talking Lora and I decided that we will get married first, because we are not going on a Honeymoon in the near future. We have traveled enough for a long time. One of you girls will have to wait until the other gets back from their Honeymoon.

"How about you, Dad?" said Grace. "I don't think it is normal for a daughter to be Maid of honor is it?"

"I don't see why not," said Sarah. "But, I have a better idea. Dad, don't you think considering how close you are with Bill and Sally that you should consider them in this picture?"

"That sounds great to me," said Lora. "I want to get to know them. John told me how much he cares for them. I think it is a good Idea, don't you John?" before John could answer he saw them coming into the rear porch.

"Come on in," said John as they came to the rear door. How are you guys?"

"We are fine," said Sally. "It looks like the whole gang is here." John introduced his girls and their fiancés. He then introduced Lora.

"So we finally get to meet Lora," said Sally. "John has been driving us crazy worrying and asking us help him find you."

"That's so sweet," said Lora kissing John on the cheek.

"I don't think you are aware that we are planning on three weddings," said John, "Grace and Paul, Sarah and Bob, and Lora and me."

"Sally," said Lora. "I think it is very important that you and I spend the next couple of days together. Perhaps we could go shopping together. I'm sure we both need some new cloths."

"I would like that," said Sally. "John has told us so much about you that I'm looking forward to getting to know you. After all we will be neighbors. But why do you say it is very important?"

"Because I want you to be my Maid-of-Honor, and John wants Bill to be his Best man." Bill and Sally got very excited.

"That would be so wonderful," said Sally with tears in her eyes.

"We would be so honored," said Bill. "I'm speechless."

"Well," said John. "The ham is about ready to eat. We can discuss the details later. Right now what I think we need is a big group hug." All nine of them got into one big group hug. There was so much affection in that group, that it made one wonder if anywhere else on the earth, there was so much love in one room as there was in this room at this moment.

The End

CPSIA information can be obtained
at www.ICGtesting.com
Printed in the USA
LVOW12s1921040517
533289LV00012B/49/P

9 781640 690547